Jackie Ashenden write... alpha heroes who've ju... only to have it blown w... heroines. She lives in A... her husband, the inimita~~b~~le Dr Jax, two kids and two rats. When she's not torturing alpha males and their gutsy heroines she can be found drinking chocolate martinis, reading anything she can lay her hands on, wasting time on social media, or being forced to go mountain biking with her husband. To keep up to date with Jackie's new releases and other news sign up to her newsletter at jackieashenden.com.

If you liked *Ruined*, why not try

Sweet Thing by Nicola Marsh
My Royal Temptation by Riley Pine
Make Me Want by Katee Robert

Discover more at millsandboon.co.uk

RUINED

JACKIE ASHENDEN

MILLS & BOON

First Published in Great Britain 2018
by Mills & Boon, an imprint of HarperCollins*Publishers*
1 London Bridge Street, London, SE1 9GF

© 2018 Jackie Ashenden

ISBN: 978-0-263-93211-9

MIX
Paper from
responsible sources
FSC **FSC® C007454**

This book is produced from independently certified FSC™ paper
to ensure responsible forest management.
For more information visit www.harpercollins.co.uk/green.

Printed and bound in Spain
by CPI, Barcelona

To Jenny.

You've been waiting so patiently for the end of Cat and Smoke's story

and here it is at last.

Hope you like it. :-)

CHAPTER ONE

Cat

IT'S ALWAYS BAD when you're in the kind of trouble that requires the help of an outlaw motorcycle club. It's especially bad when you know you'll do anything to get that help.

But what do you do when your kid's in danger? You fight any demons, slay any dragons. It's hard when you can't slay those dragons on your own, though. When you have to pay in order to have them slain for you.

I would have paid anything to get Annie away from her father.

Which was why I'd ended up standing outside the Knights of Ruin MC's clubhouse, in the rain, at midnight on a Saturday. In the middle of one of the loudest parties I'd ever heard.

I didn't want to go in. I always swore I wouldn't.

But when the devil has your kid, and the cops think everything's fine, what the hell are you supposed to do? There was only one person who could help me, and unfortunately he was inside.

Dane Kingsolver, aka Smoke, my best friend since I was a kid and a Knights enforcer.

Who was not answering his goddamn phone.

The Knights' clubhouse was in an old brick warehouse on the outskirts of Brooklyn. There were hogs lined up like toys outside, a couple of prospects hanging around looking after them, a couple more on the door. Music blared—the hard-driving beat of heavy rock. A bunch of girls were talking to the prospect on the door, their hair in artfully styled manes, their skirts up to their navels. All looking for a piece of danger, of wildness.

Idiots. They didn't know the real danger they were getting themselves into, and I almost wanted to go over there and tell them. But I didn't. They wouldn't listen. I'd done it enough times to know that.

As they disappeared inside I walked up to the prospect, who was standing with his hands in the pockets of his low-slung jeans, probably thinking he was God because he got to say who got in and who stayed out. He was young, with pretty blue eyes and still a hint of softness around his mouth.

That wouldn't last long. Soon he'd be a monster like all the rest.

He eyed me suspiciously, clearly not knowing who I was. Not that he would. I never came down here if I could help it.

I met his gaze—never look away from a snarling dog. 'I need to see Smoke.'

My voice sounded flat and definitely don't-fuck-with-me. Don't give them an opening, because the next thing you know you're on your knees with two black eyes, your dignity and strength in pieces on the floor.

Never again. Never *fucking* again.

The prospect looked even more suspicious. 'Who's asking?'

'Cat. Cat Livingston.'

The kid's gaze took me in and I knew what he was seeing. A frazzled-looking older woman in skinny jeans and a faded Ramones T-shirt. No make-up. Stained sneakers with the rubber coming off at the toe.

Unimpressive. Deeply unimpressive.

I didn't give a shit. I wasn't here to impress him. I was here to see Smoke. To save my kid. Because if there was one thing I knew, it was that Smoke loved that kid nearly as much as I did and he'd do anything for her. He'd do anything for me, too—we had each other's backs like that.

'Yeah… See, I don't know you,' the prospect said, 'And I don't fucking think—'

'I don't care *what* you think.' I cut him off curtly. 'I'm Smoke's best friend, and he's going to be pissed if you don't let me in right now.'

I didn't want to tell him about Annie. I felt like a big enough fool as it was, without this asshole knowing all about my business.

'Hey, watch your mouth,' the prospect growled, full of his own self-importance. 'Show a little goddamn respect.'

Great. So I was going to be put in my place by a teenage asshole while my violent ex had my kid. And all because of a little 'respect'. Typical biker.

I'd opened my mouth to tell him what he could do with his goddamn respect when Tiger came out through the doors, cigarette in one hand, beer in the other. Tiger was one of Smoke's best buddies, tall and leanly muscled like Smoke. He had dark, almost-black hair that glinted with copper in some lights and strange amber eyes that had apparently given him his road name.

Tiger was an asshole, but he was less of an asshole than this idiot in front of me.

'Hey, Cat,' Tiger said as he spotted me, his deep voice rough. 'What's brought you down here?'

Ignoring the prospect, I looked over at Tiger, who was standing at the top of the steps. 'Is Smoke around? I need to see him. It's urgent.'

I didn't particularly want to talk to Tiger about Annie either. He was opinionated about a lot of things, and kids was one of them.

Tiger leaned against the doorframe, lifted his beer and took a sip. He looked casual, but the gleam in his amber eyes was anything but. 'Yeah, he's around. But I don't know if you'd want to see him right now.'

'Why not? Like I said, it's urgent.' I shifted on my feet, not wanting to give away too much. 'Like…life or death urgent.'

'Uh-huh.' Tiger's gaze sharpened, though he kept on leaning against the doorframe lazily. 'Well, he's down the corridor. By the bedrooms.'

That was all I needed to hear. Not wanting to waste any time, I didn't spare the glowering prospect a glance as I went quickly up the steps. 'Thanks, Tiger,' I murmured as I slipped through the doors past him.

He gave a low laugh. 'Don't thank me. Just remember that this is a party. Don't blame me if you run into something you don't like.'

I should have listened to him. But I didn't. My head was too full of my kid and the asshole who'd picked her up from school and hadn't brought her back like he'd told me he would. Who wouldn't respond to my texts or calls.

Fear sat heavy and cold in my gut, but I tried to

ignore it as I stepped into the clubhouse. Panicking wouldn't help anyone—least of all Annie.

'Watch out for yourself, Cat,' Tiger called behind me. 'You know what a Knights party is like. An unspoken-for woman is fair game.'

Actually, I *didn't* know what a Knights party was like. I'd never been to one. But Smoke had told me enough about them. Lots of drinking, smoking and loud music. Drugs. Public sex.

Sounded hideous to me, but then again, I wasn't a Knight and I didn't go to parties, so it wasn't my place to judge.

Still, as I made my way down the corridor I realised I was in the thick of it now. And, yeah, I was damn well judging.

The common area of the clubhouse looked like a group of frat boys had gone wild in a huge draughty warehouse—fat black leather couches, pictures of bikes and naked women on the wall, a couple of tables covered in beer bottles. The air stank of cigarette smoke, joints and spilled beer.

There was a bar down one end, where a guy was pouring shots onto the stomach of a mostly naked girl who was laughing and in danger of overturning the shot glasses.

I headed straight through the doorway without stopping or looking around, trying not to draw the attention of the mass of leather-clad bikers sitting on the couches or standing around near the bar. There were a couple of guys over by a pool table with two very naked women who carried cues, and a few who looked like they were having a serious conversation in one corner—except the woman had her head in one lap while her hand worked the guy next him.

Jesus. Smoke hadn't been kidding about these parties.

I'd only been in the clubhouse a couple of times, but I knew where the bedrooms were and I headed straight there, with my attention firmly on the doorway that led to them. Only to be stopped by a massive dude with tats everywhere, a heavy black beard and the weirdest pale green eyes I'd ever seen.

'Big Red' the name on his cut said. The VP. I hadn't met him before, but Smoke had told me about him. Meanest motherfucker this side of Genghis Khan, apparently.

Just my luck to run into him.

'Hey, darlin', whatcha doing here?' he asked lazily. 'I ain't seen you before.'

I gave him a smile, trying to be nice. 'I'm looking for Smoke. Tiger said he was down this way.'

'Aw, you don't need to see Smoke. You can see me.'

Great—first the prospect, now this guy. Could this night get any better?

I widened my smile. 'Perhaps I could come see you afterward?'

He laughed, raised a hand and gave my chin a pinch—which I did not appreciate. 'Smoke's kinda busy at the moment, sweetheart.'

'Why? What's he doing?'

Big Red laughed again. 'He's with Hannah. He won't want to be interrupted.'

Of course. Smoke was with a woman. Well, every other guy appeared to be, so why not him?

Simmering anger coiled tight in my gut. So, not only had I been forced to come down here to beg for help during a goddamn party, I was now being forced to interrupt my best friend having sex. And all because my asshole ex, Justin, hadn't brought Annie home when he'd promised.

I caught that anger, held fast to it—because it sure as hell was better than the cold fear that lay beneath it.

Keeping the smile plastered firmly to my face, I sidestepped the massive VP. 'Oh, I think he'll appreciate an extra,' I said as I moved past him, giving him a wink.

Leaving Big Red safely behind me, I stepped through the door into the corridor beyond. It was quiet back here; the only sounds were the beat of some kind of heavy house music coming from behind one door and the groans coming from behind another.

Oh, God, please don't let him be behind *that* door.

I moved down the corridor and was wondering where the hell he was and whether I needed to start knocking on doors and embarrassing myself, when I rounded the corner.

And stopped.

Dead.

A tall figure leaned against the wall. A familiar figure. Six three. Wide shoulders. Lean hips. Hair the colour of black ink cut short and close to his skull. Cheekbones God himself would envy. A strong, hard jaw. Straight nose and straight black brows. A mouth that apparently had *sin* written all over it—at least it did according to some of my friends.

Smoke. The person I knew best in the world and who knew me best, too. Whom I'd met when I was five and he was seven and we were next-door neighbours. I was his friend the moment he jumped on his skateboard, a skinny little kid in torn jeans and scraped knees, showing off for the new girl next door.

He'd done magic on that board. He'd been like the wind—smooth and fluid and powerful. Even at seven. Right then and there I decided I was going to marry him.

I didn't, of course.

Because if I had I certainly wouldn't be here, standing in a bikers' clubhouse, watching him with his long fingers buried in the dark hair of the woman kneeling in front of him. Obviously getting a blow job.

A wave of the weirdest heat went through me. He always had women hanging around, and I'd seen him making out with them on more than one occasion and it had never bothered me. But there was something about *this* that hit me like the flame from a blowtorch.

He'd always been a quiet, guarded kind of guy. Never let anyone see what he was thinking, kept everything locked down. Even with me. And if you tried asking him about himself he'd give you a couple of sentences then turn the question back on you—which made him a great listener.

But that's why they called him Smoke. Because it was just a smokescreen, a distraction so he didn't have to talk about himself.

Yet there was no smokescreen now, and the expression on his face...

I couldn't look away.

I'd always known he was a beautiful man, but I'd never *felt* it before. Now, though, I was mesmerised by the intensity that burned in his features. By the fierce hunger that drew his impressive jaw tight and made the powerful tendons of his neck stand out.

He had his attention on the woman as if every movement she made was incredibly important, and his mouth was moving as he whispered things I couldn't hear. I found myself wondering what kind of expression would be in those dark eyes of his. Whether they would be burning with hunger, too.

And what it would be like if he looked at you that way, too.

Shit. I shoved the thought away. Hard. Smoke and I had never gone there and never would. Once, when I was about sixteen, I'd had a major crush on him, but he never gave me any hint that he felt the same way—not once.

So I'd pushed it aside, forgotten about it. And I definitely didn't want all those old feelings bubbling up again now. No fucking way.

I loved Smoke—he was my best friend. But when it came to sex, men were nothing but trouble, and I didn't want anything to do with them. Perhaps forever.

As if he'd sensed my presence, Smoke's head came up sharply, his black eyes slamming into mine.

And the weird heat that had me gripped intensified.

Holy shit. There was something in his gaze that made my knees weak for a second, that made me dizzy. Made me forget who I was.

As if he was looking at me for the first time in his life and really seeing me.

It was wrong and strange, and I didn't know how to deal with it. So I looked away, my face feeling like it was about to go up in flames.

'Cat?'

His voice was usually quiet and deep, but now there

was an edge to it, rough and husky, that made something inside me shiver.

'What the fuck are you doing here?'

I stared fixedly at the wall opposite. 'Sorry. I didn't mean to interrupt. But...I need you.'

'Christ, I'm a little busy—'

'It's Annie.'

He went silent. After a moment he muttered something to the woman kneeling at his feet. There was the sound of rustling fabric, the jingle of the chains attached to Smoke's low-slung jeans, a zipper being done up.

I tried to will the blush in my cheeks away, tried to calm the fast beating of my heart. I had no idea what was wrong with me, but whatever it was I didn't have time for it.

The woman hurried past me, giving me a pissed-off look. Clearly she didn't like being interrupted either.

'Talk to me,' Smoke said shortly.

I took a moment to calm myself, then looked back at him.

The expression on his face was the same as it always was—guarded, wary. The walls behind his dark eyes were impregnable. That fierce, hungry look was gone as if it had never been. And there was a part of me that couldn't help but be sad about that. A part that wanted to see it again.

Getting a hold of myself, I ignored that part. 'I'm sorry—I really didn't want to come out here. But it's Justin. He picked Annie up from school and was supposed to have dropped her off four hours ago. He didn't. He's not answering his phone or his texts or...'

I stopped, feeling a bubble of panic welling up inside me. I didn't want to go to pieces now, and there was something about knowing Smoke was here, that he had my back, that made the tension inside me relax.

'Hey,' he said quietly, and his familiar, deep voice eased the panicked feeling. 'It's okay. We'll get her. You tell anyone else about this?'

'No.'

'How did you get here? You got a car?'

'Yeah.' The short, flat questions calmed me even further.

'Good.' He ran one long-fingered hand over his shorn head. 'Fuck. Okay. I want you to go home and stay there. I'll go get Annie.'

I knew he'd help because he always did. Still, relief had me leaning against the wall to stop myself sliding down it. But that was the way I dealt with things. If something needed to be done I tended to focus on that to the exclusion of everything else—even my own feelings. Because feelings just got in the way.

The downside was that when I'd done what I needed to, I tended to get overwhelmed by the inrush of the emotions I'd managed to block. It probably wasn't a healthy way to deal with things, but it had got me out of a lot of bad situations in the past so I wasn't knocking it.

Smoke's gaze sharpened, his dark eyes glittering. He knew when I was crashing.

'You need a lift home? I'll get Tiger to take you.'

Part of me wanted to go with Smoke, but I knew he wouldn't want me getting in the way. Still, I wasn't going to collapse like a complete loser.

'No, it's okay. I've got my car.' My throat tightened, a wave of fear hollowing out my stomach. 'I just want her home, Dane. Please.'

Panic had made me use his given name, and even

though he hated it when I did, the look in his eyes softened.

Lifting one of those large, warm hands, he touched my cheek—light, fleeting. 'It's okay, kitten. I'll get her back.'

Kitten. When I called him Dane he called me kitten. A stupid joke.

Yet for the first time ever the touch and the dumb pet name sent a strange shiver straight through me.

He didn't seem to notice as he dropped his hand. 'Jesus, why the fuck is he doing this? He knows I'll fucking kill him if he so much as touches you or Annie.'

I dismissed the shiver. I really didn't need any more weirdness tonight.

'I don't know. He seemed fine when he dropped her home last week.'

Justin had been quiet for weeks, with the threat of a restraining order keeping him in line. He was a lawyer, and he was always talking about how he could get around it, but he hadn't done anything—much to my relief.

Then again, if Smoke went and got Annie and some shit went down...

'Don't do anything stupid, okay?'

I hooked a finger into one of his belt loops, holding him in case he decided to take off without listening to me. He never had before, but I wanted to be sure. He viewed Annie as a surrogate daughter and was hugely protective of her.

'I know Justin's a dick, but he could make life difficult for you.' I didn't add that he could also make life difficult for the rest of the Knights, too, but I didn't need to.

Smoke looked down at me, his face unreadable. 'He'll get what's coming to him, Cat. Nothing you can do to stop it. Especially if he tries pulling any more of this kind of shit.'

I swallowed, my throat dry all of a sudden. 'It's not him I'm worried about.'

Something shifted in his guarded dark eyes, but I couldn't tell what it was.

'Yeah, I know. Don't worry.'

He smiled. and I knew then that he was furious. Because he only ever smiled like that when he was angry.

'I'll let him live.'

And for the second time that night I shivered.

CHAPTER TWO

Smoke

I'D KILL FOR that kid. I'd kill for Cat.

And as I headed out of the clubhouse and got on my bike I wanted to. Wanted to wrap my hands around that motherfucker Justin's neck and choke the living shit out of him.

He'd never pulled anything like this before, and I knew it was a bad sign. So far he'd kept his hands off Annie, but it was only a matter of time. Pricks like that were all the same—and I should know since I'd grown up with one.

As I slammed up the kick stand Tiger came over. He looked stoned, which was unsurprising given the smell of weed wafting around the clubhouse entrance.

'Whatcha doing?'

'Cat's got a problem with Annie,' I said shortly. 'Going to deal with it.'

'Need a hand?'

'Nope.'

The fewer people involved with this the better. Especially if that fancy-ass fucking lawyer was going to start throwing his weight around. He was the son of the local police chief, and that was the only reason he was still walking around and breathing.

Keep, the Knights' president, didn't want any situations escalating with the cops since the Knights had got them sweet a year or so ago. A few favours here, a few favours there and they left us alone.

The chief's son ending up dead would kill that arrangement.

Which was a big fucking pity for me.

He'd hurt Cat once before—hurt her real bad. I'd have killed him for that alone and screw the fucking peace agreement if she hadn't told me to back off.

I'd never understood that. But she was my friend and I didn't want to fuck up her life any more than it was already.

'Sure?'

Tiger liked to be involved when shit went down, but tonight he could stay here. He'd had too much to smoke anyway.

'I'm sure.' I started up my Harley, the roar of the pipes filling the night air. 'But keep an eye on your phone in case I need backup.'

He gave me a salute with two fingers near his forehead and I took off, heading out onto the streets.

I knew where Justin lived. Sometimes I used to ride past his townhouse just to remind him that I was out there, looking for an excuse to end him. A warning to stay away from the two people I cared about most in the world.

What the fuck he was doing with Annie tonight, I did not know. But one thing was for sure: he'd made the biggest fucking mistake of his life.

I must have got lucky or something, because as I

pulled up to the kerb outside his house, the door opened and out the prick came—Annie in one arm, the handle of a giant suitcase bumping down the stairs in the other.

He didn't see me at first, obviously in a hurry to get both the kid and the suitcase into the back of his fancy BMW. So I gave him five minutes to let him think he was going to get away. Then I got off my bike, walked up to the car as he was closing the door after him, and wrenched it open before he could get it shut.

'What the hell?'

He looked up at me from his place in the driver's seat, his face a mask of rage. That soon turned to fear as I leaned an elbow casually on the roof of the car, my other arm on the open door to stop him from getting out.

'Hey, Justin,' I said, smiling. 'Going somewhere?'

His mouth twisted. 'Get away from the car or I'll call the police.'

I laughed. 'Yeah… See, I don't think you want to do that.'

'Smoke!' Annie was wriggling in her car seat. She was six and didn't know her daddy was an asshole. 'Why are you here? It's really late and we're going on a trip. Just Daddy and me!'

'Hey, kiddo.' I kept my voice low and friendly, at the same time giving her a quick scan. She looked fine, grinning at me in that way she always did, like she was having the time of her life. 'How's it hanging back there?'

She giggled. 'Nothing's hanging. Is Mom coming soon?'

'Soon, honey.'

I glanced back at her father. The guy was furious, his

mouth gone tight and mean. Cat had told me once that she thought he was good-looking, but I couldn't see it.

'Annie needs to come home now,' I said flatly. 'You unstrap her, give her to me, and nothing else'll happen.'

'Like hell.' Justin reached for the keys. 'She's *my* goddamn kid, and I'll do what I goddamn like with her!'

Fuck. The prick just didn't listen, did he?

I leaned in and grabbed the keys before he could move, pulling them out of the ignition and throwing them as hard as I could over to the other side of the street. 'Go fetch, motherfucker.'

Justin looked like he was going to explode. 'Touch her and—'

'You'll what?' I cut him off, sick of this bullshit. 'Go running to Daddy? Hide behind your fucking laws? Or are you actually going to man up and take a swing at me?'

I wished he'd take the swing. I wanted an excuse to punch him so bad it was like a pain in my gut.

But it was like he knew—like he could see how much I wanted to do it—because he suddenly leaned back in his seat, all the tension bleeding out of him.

'All right,' he said. 'Take her home, then. But you can tell Cat that I'll be back.' The asshole had the gall to grin at me. 'With a court order.'

I wanted to choke him then and there, but of course I couldn't. Keep would kill me if I fucked up the situation we had with the cops, and I wasn't that stupid. Even one punch to his face was out of bounds.

A chill went down my spine.

Justin had never actually threatened to get custody of Annie before, and Cat had always said that was because he'd never wanted her in the first place. That the only

reason he kept insisting on his parental rights was to hurt
Cat. And I believed her. The guy had major control issues, and I knew because I had the same deal.

Except there was one difference between him and
me. I'd never hurt a woman like he did and I'd never
use a kid like he used Annie.

I gave him a grin back—the kind that promised his
early death. 'Do it. If you think you can.'

He seemed to think this was the ace up his sleeve, or
something, because his smile turned smug.

'Oh, I will—don't worry. Any judge in the country
will grant me sole custody…especially against a single
mom and her dangerous biker boyfriend.'

Only long years of control kept the grin on my face
and my gun in my pocket. Otherwise I'd have put a bullet through his fucking head.

So he was going to use me against Cat.

You always knew this would happen.

Yeah, I always did. I always knew that somehow,
someday, the shit was going to hit the fan.

Cat always hated the club—hated that I was a
Knight—and, given her background, I couldn't blame
her. But until now it hadn't really come between us
because she didn't associate herself with club doings.

But now…

Jesus. How ironic that the most galling thing about
this was the fact that I wasn't even her boyfriend—
though every part of me wanted to be.

The rage started way down low in my gut, working
its way through my veins. It would have to come out
soon, but I had ways and means of doing that. Right
now all I did was keep on smiling at the piece of shit

sitting smug in his car. Imagining the death that was coming to him.

'You do that, Justin.' I made sure he heard the threat in my voice. 'And you'll get what's coming to you. No mistake. By the way, where were you going? You know it's illegal to break the custody agreement, right?'

He just laughed. 'It'll be legal soon enough. Hey, Annie. Are you ready to go see Mommy, honey?'

Annie, who'd been silent in the back, nodded. She wouldn't pick up the really adult vibes, but she'd know something was up. She was a perceptive kid.

'We're not going anywhere now?'

'Nope,' I said, before Justin could speak. 'Wanna go for a ride on my bike?'

'Yeah!'

I got Annie out myself, ignoring her father as he said his goodbyes. Then I grabbed her backpack and stowed it in the saddlebag on the bike, leaving Justin to go scrabbling around in the street for his keys.

Sitting her up in front of me, she grabbed onto my arms without me having to tell her. She'd been riding on the Harley almost since before she could talk, so she knew what to do.

I texted Cat to let her know I had Annie, then we roared out of there.

Fifteen minutes and we were at Cat's run-down apartment building. Yeah, it wasn't the greatest place to raise a kid, but she had good neighbours and the apartment itself was clean and tidy. She was a great mom and, really, that's all that counts for a kid. Annie had clean clothes, food, a bed at night and people who loved her. People who didn't beat the shit out of her. And that's plenty more than a lot of kids had.

Cat was waiting out front, her hands in the pockets of her jeans, trying to look casual, but I knew she wasn't. As I pulled up the bike she ran down the stairs, taking them two at a time to get to us.

'Hey, honey,' she said as she picked Annie up. 'How was Daddy's?' She didn't act panicked, but I could hear the sound of it in her voice anyway.

Annie didn't seem to notice, chattering on about what she'd done that afternoon.

Cat didn't say anything to me, but she didn't need to. The look she gave me out of those big green eyes of hers said it all.

I followed them up the stairs after I'd got Annie's stuff out from the saddlebag of the bike and into her apartment. Cat didn't bother to ask me any questions, too busy murmuring to Annie about how she needed to get into her pyjamas and brush her teeth because it was late.

I let her do all the kid shit first, going into the tiny, scrupulously clean kitchen and pulling open the fridge door. She usually kept a couple of cans of my favourite beer, and sure enough there was one on the shelf. I took it and went back out to the lounge, popping the tab as I sat down on the faded chintz couch that she kept covered with an Indian-patterned throw thing.

There was a low wooden coffee table in front of the couch and I swung my boots up on it like I always did, taking a swallow of my beer and sitting back.

I liked Cat's place. I had a room at the Knight's clubhouse, and that was cool, but I didn't have an apartment or anything. It was a choice I'd made a long time ago, but that didn't mean I didn't like coming around to Cat's and hanging out.

Cat kept the apartment homey, with all the decor shit she liked, despite the threadbare carpet and the dingy wallpaper. The most important thing, though, was that it had Cat in it.

That's why I liked it. That's why I kept coming there.

She'd been my friend since I was seven years old and with any luck she'll stay my friend for the rest of time.

As long as I didn't fuck it up.

I'd been good for years so far—no reason to think I wouldn't stay being good.

Cat finally appeared fifteen minutes later, walking into the living area with her hands in the pockets of her jeans again. She always did that when she was nervous, as if she thought her hands were going to give her away or something.

Her black hair was in a loose ponytail at the nape of her neck, all glossy and shiny like a slick of oil on a hot day. But she looked pale. Tired. There were dark circles under her green eyes and lines of strain around her full, pouty mouth.

Yeah, even tired and stressed out, she was *so* fucking beautiful.

But then she always had been.

She didn't look at me as she came around one of the ratty armchairs opposite the couch and sat down on it. In fact it seemed as if she was avoiding looking at me completely.

For a second I wondered what the problem was. Then I remembered.

The last time she'd seen me I'd been standing in the hallway with my dick in Hannah's mouth.

Ah. Fuck.

'So what went down with Justin?' Cat asked.

She still wasn't looking at me, her attention on my boots resting on her table.

For some reason I couldn't figure out, I wanted to leave them there—which was stupid. She'd been through hell tonight with Annie and didn't need me being a tool about putting my feet on her furniture.

But I didn't move them.

'Up here, kitten.'

Her gaze flickered up to mine, then away again. 'Justin, Dane?'

Yeah, she *really* didn't want to look at me. And the Dane thing... Second time that night. Definitely had something to do with that moment in the hallway.

I took another sip of my beer. I'd ask her about it after we'd cleared up the shit that had happened with her ex. No need for her to get weird about a fucking blow job, for Christ's sake.

'Looked like he was trying to make a run for it with Annie,' I said. 'When I got there he was putting her in his car.'

She was silent, looking fully at me this time, and I could see the panic in her eyes.

'Shit. I *knew* he was going to try and pull something like this—I just knew it.'

'Yeah, but that's not all.' This would be difficult for her, but she needed to know the truth. 'He's going to try for sole custody.'

She stilled. 'What? He's never wanted to before.'

'Well, he's serious now.' I held her gaze. 'He's going after you with the big guns, too. Single mom. Shitty apartment. Biker boyfriend.'

Her eyes widened, then flared with anger. 'No. Oh, *fuck*, no! He's *not* using you. The prick!'

That's what I loved about Cat. She always had my back. Always.

She shoved herself out of her chair, pacing angrily in front of the coffee table. 'Why now? He hasn't wanted this before. I don't get it. And anyway you're my friend—not my boyfriend.'

'Yeah, but that's how he's going to play it. Fuck, if I wanted my kid, I'd tell every lie I could to get them back.'

She stopped and stared at me. 'Not helping.'

'Hey, that's what he's doing. I'm just telling it like it is.'

'Well, don't.' She resumed pacing. 'This is crazy. He's doing it to hurt me. He doesn't really want Annie—he never did.'

'Why he's doing it doesn't matter. All that matters is how we stop him.'

She came to a halt again, her hands in fists at her sides. 'Yeah and how the hell are we going to do that? He's a lawyer. It'll be his word against mine.'

That was the problem. He was a fine, upstanding member of the community. A professional. No one knew he was also an abusive prick. No one except me and Cat.

The thing was, I'd already had to stand on the sidelines once to watch him take out his anger-management problems on someone I loved. I wasn't going to do it again. Still less when the person involved was a kid.

I needed to talk to Keep—see what he could do about the situation. He was friends with the police chief now, and that asshole was the chief's son. He'd be able to work something out. After all I was Keep's nephew, and he'd always told me that if I needed anything I only had to say the word.

I've never wanted to put anything on Keep—it wasn't his fault his brother was the biggest asshole ever to walk the earth. But this wasn't about me. It was about Cat and what *she* needed. And she needed something now.

'Don't worry. I'll deal with it.' I put as much authority as I could into my voice.

'What do you mean, you'll deal with it?' she demanded. 'How?'

'Doesn't matter how.'

'Bullshit.' Her whole posture was tense, almost vibrating. 'Don't give me that biker-secrecy crap—not when it involves Annie.'

I leaned forward, put my beer down on the table, then pushed myself out of the chair and came around the table to where she stood. Then I pulled her into my arms. She made an angry sound, putting her hands onto my chest and shoving, holding herself away. Her cheeks were flushed and she wouldn't look at me.

She was pissed and, hell, I understood. She was trying to protect Annie and she wanted to know what was going on. Except I wasn't going to tell her. Not until I'd worked it all out myself. Mainly because I knew she'd hate it.

Her mouth was a hard line, her body tense. It was difficult being close to her. Difficult having all that soft warmth against me. It made me feel guilty and it made me hard, both at the same time. Over the years I'd got better at hiding how I felt about her, but there were times when I couldn't quite do it—and tonight the interrupted blow job only made it worse.

Cat's familiar scent filled my head…a sweet, musky

smell like jasmine and sandalwood mixed together. Fuck knew what it was, but it always made me feel good. Made me feel like I was home. Made me want to wrap her in my arms and hold her close, put my face between her breasts and inhale her.

A bad move.

Cat had never shown any sign that she wanted me and I'd never wanted to put our friendship at risk. It was too important to me and so was she.

So I told my goddamn dick to calm the fuck down and held her like I always did. Giving her comfort the way a friend would.

'I know you're scared,' I said. 'I know you're worried. But let me help you and Annie.'

Her palms were resting on my chest and I could feel the heat of them settle right down through me, burning through my T-shirt and onto my skin. She was staring at them, and not at me, as if the backs of her hands were the most interesting things in the world.

'I don't want to involve the club,' she said quietly. 'Please, Smoke. You know how I feel about that.'

I did. But this wasn't just about her. This was about Annie, as well.

'Remember that the club hasn't done anything to you. And if they can help Annie, isn't that more important?'

'It's not… It's not about Dad.'

Sure it wasn't. Her father had been a biker and a nasty bastard. Like mine. Except *her* dad hadn't beaten her half to death every time he got drunk. No, he'd been more the absent type—away a lot on club business and not much interested in anything else. Especially not the poor little rich girl he'd got pregnant or the daughter he'd fathered.

Anyway, I called it like I saw it.

'That's a piece of shit, Cat. And you know it.'

Her body tensed and she looked up at me, her eyes sharp as green glass. 'This is about Annie, not Dad.'

'Yeah, it is.' My hands were on her hips and I found myself tightening my hold on her, as if I could make her see that her fears were all the product of her past with nothing but the strength of my grip alone. 'Which means if you want to make sure she's safe, you need to let me handle this.'

An expression I didn't recognise moved in her eyes. Anger and something else, too. Something unfamiliar. Then her gaze dipped and—holy fucking shit—she was staring at my mouth.

I went still. Completely and utterly still. She'd never done that before, and there was only one reason in the entire world she would.

Obviously picking up on my shock, she pushed at me again. But I held on. No way was I going to let her go—not now. Not when I'd caught her looking at me the way I never in a million years thought she would.

'Smoke.' She pushed harder, her cheeks flushed, her thick black lashes veiling her gaze.

'No.' I tightened my grip, suddenly desperate to know what the hell was going on. 'We need to talk, Cat.'

'What? No, we don't. Look, I'm tired and—'

'We need to talk about what you saw in the hallway tonight.'

CHAPTER THREE

Cat

I FROZE AS soon as he said the word *hallway*.

What a stupid bitch I was. I should never have looked. I should never have allowed him to get close. But he'd given me plenty of hugs before and it shouldn't have been a big deal.

Yet it was. There was something about the feel of his hands on my hips, the quiet strength in them, that I'd never noticed before. I'd never noticed how hot he was either. My hands on his chest felt scorched, like they'd been pressed against a furnace. He smelled delicious, too, his familiar aftershave reminding me of a forest—all dark and woody and spicy—along with the faintest tinge of leather from under his cut.

And when I looked up at him, angry and resistant to the idea of him going to the club for help with Annie, for some reason I couldn't hold his gaze. The darkness of his eyes seemed to draw me in, suck me down, wrap me up in soft velvet and keep me there. It disturbed me, so I looked at his mouth instead.

A big mistake. Because that wasn't any better. I couldn't help noticing how beautifully shaped it was, how full the curve of his bottom lip was, and how if anyone had a kissable mouth, then surely it had to be Smoke...

Yeah, crazy. That's what I was. Certifiable. He was my friend—my best friend—and I didn't want to look at him that way. I didn't have many people in my life who'd stuck around, but he was one of them and I did *not* want to screw that up.

So I tried to dismiss my blush through sheer force of will, tried to ignore the heat that was stealing through me at the feel of his body against mine. Tried desperately not to notice that the chest beneath my palms was rock hard and so very, *very* hot...

'What hallway?' I said stupidly.

'You know what I'm talking about.'

'Oh, that.'

I tried to pull away, but he was having none of it. His hands moved to the back pockets of my jeans, and before I could do anything to stop him, he slid them down inside them, his fingers curving over my butt.

All the breath left my lungs in a wild rush and I looked up at him in shock.

His eyes were so dark—black as tar—and they glittered, making something inside me draw in tight like a hand closing into a fist.

'What are you *doing*?' My voice sounded breathless and frightened, which was annoying since I'd never been afraid of Smoke.

He ignored me. 'You saw me getting sucked off by Hannah.'

I blushed like a teenager but bluffed it out. 'Yeah, so what? It was disgusting.'

'Is that why you're acting so weird?'

I couldn't think. All I was aware of was how hot his hands felt inside the pockets of my jeans, with his palms pressing lightly, the heat of them soaking through the denim. But that wasn't the worst part. The worst part was the heat of him in front of me and how conscious I was of it. How conscious I was of *him*.

Beneath my palms his chest felt incredibly hard— a wall of firm muscle that probably wouldn't move no matter how hard I pushed. *If* I pushed. And his arms were around me strong and sure, like bands of iron.

He'd held me in those arms before. When Dad had gone away for that final time and never come back. That final job he'd had to do for the stupid club he'd been a part of. Not that he'd ever paid much attention to Mom and me, but a death was a death and my mom wasn't the hugging type. At least, she didn't hug me. So all I had was Smoke.

But back then I didn't notice the firmness of his chest or the heat of his body. Or how good he smelled. Back then all I felt was grief and rage.

Now, though, everything was different.

'I'm not acting weird,' I mumbled, staring at his chest.

God, I so did *not* want to have this conversation with him. Not when all this awareness was careening around inside me, and most definitely not while he had his hands in my back pockets and his arms around me.

'You are. Look at me.'

I don't know what it was in his voice. A note of something…*hard*. Like it was an order. Normally I hated people telling me what to do, but right then I found myself doing it. Lifting my head and meeting his eyes.

They were black—like the extradark, extrastrong espresso I used to make him when he had a hangover. And they were just as hot, too. They made an electric shock go straight down my spine.

I shoved at him then, entirely instinctively, trying to get away from all the weird feelings...trying to get away from *him*. He let me go straight away and I had the strangest sense of disappointment as he did so, as if I'd been enjoying his hold.

You're crazy.

Yeah, I really was. I didn't have feelings for Smoke. He was the best friend I had in the world—like a damn brother. End of story.

He frowned. 'What the fuck, Cat?'

My cheeks were on fire and I really didn't want to look at him. But I made myself do it, folding my arms defensively over my chest. 'I need some space, okay?'

His dark gaze scanned my face and, damn him, he probably knew exactly why I was blushing. Jesus, how embarrassing was that?

Slowly he folded his arms, mirroring me, and I couldn't stop noticing the flex of his biceps as he did so, and the black ink of the stars cascading down his left upper arm flexing along with them.

I'd never been a fan of tattoos—not when all they ever spelled for me was bad news. But the stars on Smoke's arm suddenly seemed...fascinating, somehow. They drew my attention to the muscles there, to the tanned skin beneath the ink. Made me wonder what the rest of that skin looked like...

God, he was tall. And broad. I'd noticed that once, back when I was sixteen and crushing on him like crazy. Even at eighteen he'd been muscular and lean hipped, like a panther. Now, at thirty, he'd filled out, the cotton of his T-shirt stretching over his chest.

'Cat.' His voice had gone low and husky. 'Are you checking me out?'

You are. You're totally checking him out.

The blaze in my cheeks felt like a supernova. I should have looked him in the eye and brazened it out, but I couldn't make myself do it. Avoiding his gaze would tell him more or less the same thing of course, but it was way less confrontational. And I'd had too much confrontation tonight as it was.

'No, of course I'm not,' I snapped and turned on my heel, heading to the kitchen. 'I'm going to get a damn beer.'

Plus some space while I was at it.

In the kitchen, I pulled open the fridge and grabbed myself a can, popping the tab and taking a long, deep swallow to cool myself down.

I had no idea what the hell was going on with me. No idea why I was suddenly checking out my best friend like I hadn't had sex in years.

That's the problem. You haven't *had sex in years.*

I scowled at the cracked paint of the kitchen wall. That was unfortunately true. I hadn't. But men were such bastards and I'd had enough. I certainly had after Justin.

He'd started out so great—just the kind of guy I was after. A lawyer earning good money, on the straight and narrow. Definitely not a drug user or a criminal, like the people my dad used to associate with. In fact Justin was as far from that as it was possible to get—which was why I'd fallen for him like the proverbial ton of bricks.

It wasn't until I was pregnant and things weren't

going so well at his firm that the cracks in his good-boy facade had started to show. He'd always had a problem with anger, and when he got angry he lashed out. At me.

The first time he hit me I was so shocked I didn't know what to do. He cried and told me he was sorry, that he'd never do it again. So I forgave him. It didn't happen again until after Annie was born. Then he did it again. And again. Three times I put up with it. The fourth he nearly knocked me out.

So I left him.

Good boys were overrated… Bad boys were just like my dad. And since there was nothing in between, I took nothing. It was easier—better for me and better for Annie. After all, between her and my two jobs—the call centre during the day and Lucky's, the bar I worked at some nights—I didn't have time for men anyway.

I didn't miss them. Sex with Justin had been pretty average—certainly no better than what I could get with my own imagination and a decent vibrator. At least I was in charge of my own orgasms, which I found very satisfying.

So why were you looking at Smoke?

That was the one question I couldn't answer, though I wished I could. Because that was the very last thing I needed in my life right now.

'You gonna tell me what's going on?'

I turned sharply, my heart giving the stupidest jump at the sound of Smoke's voice.

He was standing in the kitchen doorway, one shoulder hitched up against the frame, his arms folded. His black eyes had narrowed. I'd never found that look threatening—not once. But I did now. Not because he was going to hurt me—I knew Smoke would never do that—but because he knew me. He knew that something was bothering me.

And if you're not careful he'll guess what that something is.

Shit. He would, too.

Trying for calm, I took a swig of my beer, the cold liquid putting out the strange fire burning in my veins. 'Nothing's going on,' I said. 'It's just been a hell of a night, what with Annie and—'

'And watching your best friend get blown?'

'Jesus, Smoke.' This time I managed to look him in the eye. 'How many times do you want to keep saying that?'

'I don't know. Until you stop acting weird?'

'I'm *not* acting weird. Okay, it was disconcerting, but I'm a big girl. I know what you guys get up to in the clubrooms. It's nothing I haven't seen before.'

But his narrow black stare didn't budge. Like he was seeing things in me that I didn't know were there. It was unsettling.

'And what about you checking me out?'

'I wasn't checking you out! You're my friend. You're like my damn brother. Which means if I was looking at you like that, I'd be pretty damn sick. Don't you think?'

He didn't say a word. Just kept staring at me. And I could hear the echo of my voice bouncing off the walls, high and sharp and vehement. Too vehement.

I was incriminating myself with every word I spoke.

Man, could this night get any worse?

I turned away, running a hand through my hair. 'You know what? I'm exhausted and I need to go to bed. So let's talk about this later.'

For a second I didn't think he was going to say anything, that he was going to keep standing there staring at me all night. But then he said, 'Yeah, okay. You do look tired. But, Cat?'

I glanced at him. 'What?'

Something glittered in his black eyes that made my heart race fast and hard. 'We *will* talk about this later—get me?'

I swallowed and lifted a shoulder like I didn't give a shit. 'Sure.'

He sighed, his arms dropping to his sides, and pushed away from the doorframe. 'I'll handle that prick Justin, too, okay?'

'Yeah...' I let out a silent breath. 'Thanks for getting Annie, Smoke. I mean... Just thanks.'

They were paltry words for what he'd done, but I didn't have any other way to thank him. He'd know how much I meant them, though.

He smiled and, like always, it made me feel warm inside. Made me feel really good. Like the sun had come out to sit on my shoulder.

'Anytime, kitten. Anytime.'

CHAPTER FOUR

Smoke

'HEY, PREZ. YOU got a minute?' I stood aside as one of the club hang-arounds, a brunette called Bella, sidled out of Keep's office, tugging down her skirt and doing nothing to hide the satisfied look on her face.

Keep himself was sitting at his desk, his hands loosely linked behind his head, looking extremely fucking satisfied himself. I guess there's nothing like a lunchtime screw when there isn't much else going on.

He grinned, lifting his chin at the chair opposite the desk. 'Sure. Take a seat.'

I came in and sat down, leaning my elbows on my knees.

I didn't like to ask favours of people since I hated being in debt—another thing that made me different from my old man—but Keep was different. He was my uncle, Dad's younger brother, and the man who'd protected me when he could. He'd also been the one to introduce me to the Knights, becoming president not long after I patched in.

Being in debt to Keep was okay. He was a brother; he was my president, and he had my back. He had everyone's back. That was why they called him Keep. Because he kept what was his and he didn't let it go.

He gave me a measuring look, letting the silence hang there for a bit. Then he said, 'So what's up? Something important? I can tell by the look on your face.'

It *was* important. This was Annie and Cat, and there weren't any other people on this whole fucking planet more important to me than they were.

But I had to be careful about how I was going to ask for this. Keep had a good relationship with the police chief, a relationship that was important, too—especially if you wanted to stay on the straight and narrow like Keep did. He made sure the club maintained a low profile with the law and stayed out of trouble.

Well, we weren't called the Knights in Shining Armor. We were the Knights of Ruin for a reason. But that reason didn't include drugs or whores or guns or any of that shit. We did the usual MC stuff for cash: a strip club, a couple of garages around town and a good bit of protection and hired muscle work. But we weren't in it for the money. We were in it because we wanted to ride and live free, our brothers by our side.

I was in it because the Knights were my family—certainly more of a family than my own had been—and I wanted it to stay that way. I didn't want to rock the boat.

Except this thing with Annie might just do a shitload of rocking.

I had to try, though. For Cat's sake.

'Yeah, something's up.' I met Keep's gaze. 'It's got to do with Justin Grant.'

Keep's blue eyes narrowed. 'Campbell Grant's son?'

'Unfortunately.'

He sighed and unlinked his hands, sitting forward in his chair, folding his arms and leaning his elbows on the desk. 'Fuck's sake, Smoke. Not again.'

I fought a hot rush of irritation. Everyone knew I hated Grant's guts because of Cat, and that if I'd had my way I would have put him in the ground with no regrets if I could have got away with it. But I'd never actually put a move on him. So Keep getting pissed at me was annoying.

Still, I knew where Keep was coming from.

Yet this was Cat. And that was a whole other story.

So I swallowed my anger, kept my posture loose and held his gaze steadily. 'If it was just about Grant being a dick, I'd agree with you. But last night he didn't return Annie, and when I caught up with them I found him putting her into a car with a big suitcase.' I paused. 'He didn't look like he was planning on coming back, Keep.'

There was no expression at all on Keep's face. He was good at hiding his emotions.

'So? He's the kid's father.'

Keep knew all about Cat and Annie. He knew Cat was the only thing that kept me sane, the only bright spot in the entire damn world when things had got really dark. He knew what she meant to me and he knew why this was important.

The motherfucker was playing devil's advocate.

'And Cat is Annie's mother,' I said flatly. 'He doesn't have any right to take Annie away from her.'

Keep lifted a shoulder. 'Sounds like custody drama to me. Let them sort it out themselves. Got nothing to do with us.'

'Grant's going to come back,' I went on, ignoring him. 'He's promised to get a court order giving him sole custody. And because he's a lawyer, and full of shit, he's going to tell them about Cat working nights and about how she's got a biker boyfriend, that it's dangerous for Annie to be around her.'

'Yeah, okay. I hear you. But, again, what's that got to do with us?' Keep's stare was sharp. 'I know Cat's important to you, but this isn't club business. I got a whole lot of things going on now, and I don't need any attention from the police. If the club gets involved with this…'

Frustration rose, but I swallowed it down, playing it cool. 'I know all that. But we have to do something. That prick hurt Cat. And I'll be damned if he does it again.'

Keep let out a breath. 'She's your friend—I get it. And the kid is cute. No doubt about it. But I'm saying no. We can't afford the heat it would bring down. Not now.'

Fuck. If it had been anyone else, I would have let it go. But it wasn't anyone else. It was Cat. And I hadn't been able to protect her from Justin last time, which meant I was *not* going to fail again.

'Keep,' I said clearly, levelly. 'I've never asked you for anything. Not one single fucking thing. Not even when that shit went down with Dad. But I'm asking you now. I need you to help Cat and Annie.'

Keep's blue eyes turned cold. He was an easygoing guy on the surface, but that only went so far. There was a reason he was club president, and it wasn't because he was a walkover.

'No.' His voice was very quiet. 'That's my final answer. I'm not saying it again.'

I knew that tone. It was his presidential do-not-fuck-

with-me tone. No one argued with that—not if they
liked their balls hanging where they were.

But I had a line, too. And Cat was it.

'If they were ours, you would, right?' A stupid question, since it should have gone without saying. I had to
check, though.

'You know I would. But they're not.'

No, they weren't.

Yet.

I leaned back in my chair, an idea going around and
around in my head. Because that motherfucker Justin
was *not* going to hurt her again. Over my dead fucking body.

Luckily, there was another option.

Unluckily, Cat was going to hate it.

There was only one way to make Cat and Annie
part of the Knights, and that was for me to take her as
my old lady.

I couldn't deny that it was something I'd wanted for
years—a secret fantasy that wouldn't ever make it into
reality since Cat didn't feel that way about me. But,
shit, we could fake it, couldn't we? Make it look like
we were together at least enough for the rest of the MC
to believe it and protect her, if and when Grant came
gunning for her.

Are you sure she doesn't feel that way about you?

I blinked, the thought hitting me hard. Where the
hell had that come from? Admittedly her behaviour last
night had been weird—not looking me in the eye and
getting all strange and tense when I got near her. Then,
when I'd brought up the topic of that blow job, she'd
blushed. Like she was the one embarrassed about it.

Still, discussing your best friend's blow job would be pretty embarrassing for a chick.

So why did you put your hands in the pockets of her jeans?

I shifted uncomfortably in the chair.

Never in all the years we've been friends had I touched her like that. In fact I'd never made one single move on her, even though sometimes I wanted to so bad I was like a junkie in search of a fix. She was my friend. End of. Besides, I knew how she felt about MCs.

To say she wasn't the Knights' greatest fan was a severe understatement.

Anyway, I still didn't know what had made me slide my hands into the back pockets of her jeans, feel the heat of her against my palms, pull her close. She was trying to avoid me and I simply wanted to hold her there so we could talk about it.

Yeah, sure. You fucking liar.

I shifted again, my palms stinging from the memory. Fuck, she'd felt hot. Then she'd put her hands on my chest and it was like I'd been plugged into a goddamn wall socket. She'd touched me plenty of times before and it had never felt like that—mainly because I'd trained myself to ignore my reactions around her.

She'd been blushing, too. Had touching me *done* something for her?

'Jesus, Smoke,' Keep muttered. 'You got a problem or something? You're shifting around like a two-year-old needing the potty.'

Mother fuck. If I wasn't careful Keep was going to notice something else, because my dick was starting to think interesting things about why Cat might have been blushing. And why she'd suddenly pushed me away as if I'd burned her.

Why she'd been so weird about not wanting to discuss that blow job.

Christ. Getting a hard-on in the absence of any naked chicks, while sitting talking your president, wasn't exactly a good look.

Shoving thoughts of her and how she'd felt in my arms away, I pushed myself out of my chair. 'Nope. No problem.'

'I'm sorry about Cat.' Keep looked it, too, but he had the club as a whole to consider and I understood that. 'We good?'

'All good, Prez.'

And we would be. Because I'd made my decision.

There was only one way to protect her and Annie from her dick ex and that was to make her mine.

Cat wasn't going to like it, but I'd talk her around. I'd convince her. This was all for Annie's sake, and nothing was more important than making sure she was safe.

CHAPTER FIVE

Cat

I WAS FINISHING up my shift at Lucky's when the door opened with a bang and Smoke strode in.

Carl, who owned Lucky's Bar, wasn't a fan of the Knights, and he didn't much like Smoke and the other brothers hanging around. He could make life difficult for me when he was in the mood, so Smoke tended to steer clear of Lucky's whenever I was working.

Though tonight it looked as if he had something important to say.

Dear God, if it was about that blow job again, I'd get security to haul his ass out of there myself.

'Hey, Cat.'

His deep, husky voice rolled over me as he approached the bar and I had no idea why I found myself staring at him like a complete idiot. Because there was no reason to stare—none at all. Not when he was dressed like he normally was, in black boots, worn black jeans and a faded black T-shirt, his cut over the top. Nothing special, nothing fancy.

Yet I couldn't take my eyes off him.

Looking at how the cotton of his T-shirt pulled over

the hard muscles of his chest and biceps, how the waist-band of his jeans sat low on his lean hips, how one corner of his mouth curved in a sexy half smile, how black his eyes were and how they drew me in, made me feel like I was drowning.

What was wrong with me? It was like he was projecting some kind of electric field, sensitising my skin, making it prickle with awareness and a heat that was totally unwelcome.

No. Just no. The weirdness of a couple of nights ago was fresh in my mind, and I'd been hoping that it would have all gone away and everything would be like it was.

Seemed I was destined for disappointment.

Smoke leaned his elbows on the bar and raised an eyebrow without saying anything.

I jerked my gaze away, busying myself with folding some of the cleaning cloths we kept behind the bar for drying glasses.

'What are you doing here?' The question came out quick and graceless, but I couldn't seem to moderate my tone.

If he took offence, or even noticed, he didn't show it.

'I got to talk to you.'

'Now? I'm in the middle of work.'

'It's important.'

I folded the cloth in half, lining up the edges and making sure they met. 'Can't it wait? You know Carl doesn't like you hanging around.'

'Yeah, but, like I said, this is important. It's about Annie and you.'

I couldn't avoid his gaze any longer—avoiding it was already strange enough as it was. Bracing myself, I finally looked up and met his dark eyes.

There it was again, that electric shiver moving over my skin like static.

Crazy. He was here to talk about something important, to do with Annie and me, and all I could think about was my physical reaction to him.

I had to get a grip. I had to put this stupid…whatever it was…to one side and forget about it. I wasn't getting involved with a biker—not after the lesson my dad had taught my mom, let alone the fact that the biker in question was my best friend. So there wasn't any point fixating on this irrational attraction.

I was over men—possibly for good.

I had to let it go.

'Okay?' I leaned a hip against the bar. 'So what's the deal?'

'I've figured out a way to make sure Grant never comes near you or Annie.'

I blinked, my heart leaping inside my chest. 'Seriously?'

'I'm always serious, kitten.' He didn't smile, and there was an intense look on his face. 'Especially when it comes to you two and your safety.'

I let the *kitten* go, sagging against the bar in relief. 'How? What did you do?'

He still didn't smile, which maybe should have clued me in to the fact that what he was going to say next wasn't going to make my life any easier.

'You're not going to like it.'

The relief ebbed, my muscles tensing. 'What exactly am I not going to like?'

'It involves the Knights.'

Smoke was always like this when he was telling me stuff I didn't want to hear. Calm. Direct. Straight-up.

Laying out the unpleasant facts so I knew exactly where I stood.

'It involves you and Annie being under their protection.'

My first instinct was *no fucking way in hell*. I hated the MC and didn't want to have anything to do with them—and I *especially* didn't want any child of mine anywhere near them.

'I told you I didn't want to involve—'

'I know what you told me. But hear me out, okay?'

I bit down on my protest. I didn't want to hear him out, but if he'd gone to the trouble of figuring out a way to help Annie, then the least I could do was listen.

'Fine. So how are Annie and me going to be under their protection? We're not part of the club.'

He shifted on his feet, and if I hadn't known any better, I would have said he looked uncertain. Which was strange, because Smoke was *never* uncertain.

'Yeah,' he said. 'That's the hard part. To be under their protection you have to be a club member.'

'How? Unless they're suddenly recruiting women?' I put a little sarcasm into that last part, because obviously no outlaw MC would allow women to be full members.

Smoke ignored that, gazing at me in a very focused, very intent way. It made that electric current stronger, lifting all the hairs along the back of my neck and my forearms, making me short of breath.

'There's one way,' he murmured. 'If you're my old lady, you'll have the full protection of the club and so would Annie.'

Shock held me still. I had no idea what to say—no idea what to even think.

First there was the whole issue of the club. Then there was being his old lady... He couldn't be serious.

But he wasn't smiling. And the look in his eyes... Shit, I knew that look. He always had it when he meant to do something and he was going to do it whether I liked it or not. He'd always been a guy who liked his own way, and he got it enough that it made him unhappy when he didn't.

'You're not serious, right?' I tried to sound normal and not like a shaky little girl.

'Yeah, I'm serious.'

Of course he was. He was never anything but.

'You and me will be together as long as it takes for Grant to get off your back, but it won't be real or anything.' He stopped all of a sudden, as if he'd meant to say something else and held himself back at the last minute. 'We only have to make it look believable to the club.'

Make it look believable.

What the hell did *that* mean?

You know what it means, idiot.

Heat shot through me—a flare like a lighted match held against my skin. I tried like hell to ignore it. To concentrate on the facts instead.

'So,' I said carefully, busying myself with folding the cloths again. 'Let me get this straight. You think that if you make me your old lady, the club will protect me and Annie from Justin.'

'I don't think. I *know*.' He said it like the gospel truth, handed down from God himself.

'I thought your president didn't want to get on the wrong side of the police chief. If Justin comes after Annie and the club stops him...' I let the sentence hang.

'Checked it out with Keep this morning.' Smoke put his hands flat on the bar. 'He won't lift a finger if you're not part of the Knights. But if you're one of us, you'll have an army at your back. Club comes first, and the chief can go fuck himself.'

Club comes first.

Wasn't that the lesson I'd learned all through my childhood? That the club, the brothers were the most important things in my father's life.

My mother had learned that lesson, too, when she was still a silly socialite, falling for a badass biker with tats on his arms and a gleaming Harley. She'd thought he was going to give her the freedom from her wealthy family that she'd always craved. Instead he'd given her a one-way ticket to Junkieville.

He never married her—never made her his old lady. He got her pregnant, then left her in a shitty apartment trying to bring up his kid by herself because her family had cut her off. And the only reason she'd stayed was because he kept her in drugs.

Oh, yeah, and apparently she loved him, even though he used to hit her sometimes.

A real prince, my dad.

To this day I have no idea why he didn't make her his old lady. It was like he thought we weren't good enough to be part of his precious club—like it was far too special to share with us. Not that we *wanted* to be part of it… Or at least I didn't.

I hated him and, because of its influence on him, I hated that club.

I hated the Knights for their influence on Smoke, too. The day he told me he was going to sign up to be a prospect I didn't speak to him for two whole weeks. I didn't want him to join. I didn't want them to take him away from me.

We got over that years ago, but sometimes I still felt the betrayal of it.

Like now.

'Cat.' Carl's voice behind me was mean with annoyance. 'You've still got fifteen minutes. Get back to work.'

Smoke pushed himself sharply back from the bar.

'Don't—' I began.

But it was too late.

'She's finishing early tonight.'

Smoke's voice had that hard, flat quality it got whenever he was giving orders. Or stating facts. Or making decisions. Not that there was any difference between them.

'Excuse me?' Carl sounded pissed. 'Are *you* her fucking boss?'

'Smoke, don't.' The last thing I needed was trouble with Carl. It was shitty work, and the pay was terrible, but I needed it. Especially when my day job barely paid the bills.

But Smoke ignored me, digging his wallet out of the back pocket of his jeans and grabbing a couple of bills out of it. He tossed the bills down on the bar.

'Here. Her pay for the last fifteen minutes of her shift.' His black gaze shifted to me. 'Come on. We need to talk.'

I glanced at the money on the bar—I really did get paid shit—then turned to Carl.

'Carl, look,' I said. 'Smoke didn't—'

'I don't care what he did or didn't do. I told you I didn't want him hanging around here, and yet here he is.' Carl grimaced, then jerked his head towards the exit. 'Go on—get out of here.'

'But I—'

'And don't come back.'

Anger flared inside me. Wonderful. Not only did I have Justin making threats to take Annie away from me, and Smoke wanting to protect me by involving me in his goddamn MC, now I had to find myself another job.

Life was just getting better and better.

Swallowing the few choice words I wanted to level at both Carl *and* Smoke, I set my jaw, collected my purse and strode out from behind the bar. I headed towards the exit, not bothering to look behind me to see if Smoke was following.

Slamming open the door, I stepped out onto the street, then headed straight towards the bus stop.

'Cat—wait up.'

I didn't.

Frustrated rage burned in my gut. Rage at the world for the situation I was in, for all the decisions I'd made in good faith that had turned out to be really shitty ones that had not only put me at risk, but also my kid.

I thought Justin was one of the good guys. Clean-cut and earning good money—not some low-life asshole like my dad. I wasn't going to be like my mother, attaching myself to some man because I was desperate for drugs or love or whatever other crap people get needy over.

I was going to fall for a *good* man and we'd have a *good* life together. Have great kids and a nice place and a fulfilling career.

Instead all I got were black eyes, a shitty apartment and a hand-to-mouth existence.

There was only one good thing I'd got from Justin and that was Annie. Now she was under threat, and there wasn't a damn thing I could do about it. I hated being so helpless. It brought back all those crappy feelings I'd had when Justin first showed his true colours. Of powerlessness. Of worthlessness. Of weakness.

I'd promised myself never again, and yet somehow he still had the power to hurt me.

'Cat.' Warm fingers wound around my arm and held on, bringing me up short. *'Stop.'*

I halted, keeping my gaze on the bus stop ahead of me. 'Thanks for making me lose my job, Smoke,' I said. 'I'm sure I really don't need that money.'

'It was a shitty job anyway.' He sounded completely unrepentant. 'And I have money if you need it.'

Arrogant son of a bitch.

I turned to look at him, his handsome face shadowed by the streetlight behind him. The intense look in his eyes hadn't faded one iota, making me feel restless and shaky, wanting something I couldn't put a name to.

'The money isn't the point,' I said. 'You made me lose my job, and I'm not feeling very happy about that right now.'

'Sure, you're pissed about the job, but tell it like it is, Cat. You don't like my idea.'

'About being your old lady? Of *course* I don't like it. I think it's stupid.'

Something crossed his face—I didn't know what it was. Maybe hurt or disappointment or a combination of both. And his mouth hardened. He didn't often get pissed with me, but I knew when he was. Like now.

'Yeah, well, maybe you should stop being so fucking one-eyed about the club.' There was a dangerous edge to his voice. 'Maybe you should stop thinking about your own issues for a change and start thinking about Annie's.'

Anger flared inside me, hot as a Fourth of July bon-fire. I'd just lost my job because of him, and now he was telling me I wasn't thinking of *my kid*?

Everything I did was for her. *Everything.*

'Don't you dare tell me I'm not thinking of her just because you're pissed that I didn't like your idea.' I jerked my arm out of his hold, too angry with him to think about what I was saying. 'She's *my* kid—not yours. You're not her father. You don't get a say!'

CHAPTER SIX

Smoke

I FELT LIKE she'd kicked me straight in the balls. The pain was so bright, so raw. I acted on instinct, taking her by her forearms and spinning her around, pushing her up against the brick wall of the building next to us and holding her there.

'You'd really say that to *me*?' I couldn't keep the pain out of my voice. 'Fuck you, Cat. I knew that kid before she was born. I spent more time with her than Justin did. Hell, I'm more a father to her than he ever fucking was. So don't you *dare* tell me I don't get a say!'

Her eyes had gone very wide, the green in them darkening as she stared at me in shock. Like she saw a stranger standing there instead of me.

Like Justin maybe? Have you got more of your old man in you than you thought?

I went cold. No way. No fucking way.

Letting her go, I stepped back and turned away, trying to get a goddamn grip.

I knew Cat was angry—and yeah, putting that asshole boss of hers in his place and getting her fired hadn't been my best move. But Annie was a daughter to me in so many ways that it hurt to be told I had no right to help her.

So Cat had issues with the club. After what her old man had put her and her mom through, I couldn't blame her. But the Knights were different from the MC her dad had been in, and I sure as hell wasn't *him*.

You're just pissed she didn't fall gratefully into your arms when you told her your idea.

Couldn't deny it—there was a part of me that wanted that badly. That hoped she'd put her arms around me, tell me that being my old lady was what she'd been dreaming about all her life.

Yeah, I was fucking toast for her, and the fact that she hadn't done any of that only added to the pain.

'Smoke?'

Cat's voice was behind me—not so angry this time, more uncertain.

I didn't reply, not trusting myself not to say something stupid and make things worse.

There was a feather-light touch on my back, brief and over far too fast.

'I'm sorry. I shouldn't have said that. You *do* get a say. I'm just… You know I don't like the club and you know why. And this whole situation with Annie is scaring the shit out of me.'

Typical Cat. She blew up like a volcano when she was scared.

My normal thing would have been to turn around and give her a hug, tell her she didn't need to be afraid, that all she needed to do was trust me. But she'd got me where it hurt and I was still pissed.

You know what you want to do.

Yeah, I totally did. I wanted her to get down on her

knees and apologise the old-fashioned way. With my dick in her mouth.

Another light pressure on my back and this time it was staying there.

'Smoke? Please. I didn't mean it. You know I didn't.'

But that was the thing. I didn't know. Because she was right. Annie wasn't my kid. Either Cat or that asshole Justin could take her away and there would be nothing I could do about it.

The light pressure increased as her palm settled between my shoulder blades.

'I wish you were her father. You're a damn sight better dad than Justin ever was.'

If I had been Annie's father, we wouldn't be standing here right now. I'd be at Cat's place and Cat would be naked under me.

Something hardened in me at the thought, and for once it wasn't my damn dick.

This was going to happen. Cat was going to be my old lady, and I didn't care if she didn't want to be or not. She was a grown woman and she could make her own decisions, sure, but Annie was still a kid and she needed protection. Which meant if Cat was going to let her own issues get in the way of helping her kid, I was going to call bullshit on them.

I turned around, the warmth of her hand lingering between my shoulder blades, making me ache. But I kept my expression hard.

She stared at me uncertainly, looking so fucking hot in the tight green Lucky's T-shirt she always wore to work. The one that clung to her tits and made me want to gather them in my hands, feel the weight of them against my palms, stroke her nipples through the fabric and watch them get hard.

Maybe you should do that. See what happens.

Fuck, that voice in my head was playing devil's advocate. I shouldn't listen to it.

'It's going to happen, Cat,' I said aloud. 'I'm not standing by and letting that prick get his hands on you or Annie—not again. Understand me?'

Her expression closed up, her pouty mouth flattening. 'I don't—'

'What?' I interrupted, folding my arms. 'You got a better idea?'

The look on her face became guarded, wary, and I knew why. She wasn't seeing me as a friend right now. She was seeing me as a hard-ass biker putting pressure on her.

Maybe that was for the best, though. Maybe she'd been seeing me as a friend for far too long.

'No,' she said quietly. 'I don't.'

'Then it's on. I'll take you as my old lady and if Justin comes after Annie again, he'll have the whole fucking club to deal with.'

Her throat moved as she swallowed, and I watched it, wanting my hand on it. Wanting to feel her pulse beneath my palm. Wanting to feel it get faster as I leaned in to take her mouth.

Christ, I was losing it. And there was a part of me that didn't give a shit. As if it had been waiting for this opportunity all this time—this chance to take her like I'd always wanted to. But I couldn't listen to that part of myself.

Cat had been burned—and burned very badly—and

getting physical with her just because my dick was getting impatient would be a mistake.

She looked away, as if she knew exactly the kind of
thoughts that had been sitting in my head, and there
was a long silence.

Then she said, 'I'm not moving into that clubhouse
with you and neither is Annie—okay?'

I let out a slow, silent breath. She was going for it.
She was fucking *going* for it. But I didn't relax, holding her wary gaze with mine. I wanted to hear her say
the word out loud.

'Was that a yes, kitten?'

Irritation flashed in her gaze. 'Christ, Smoke, I'm
not going to—'

'Say it.' I hadn't meant it to sound like an order, but
it came out as one all the same.

I saw something spark in those big green eyes—a
reaction I was positive she hadn't meant me to see. A
gleam of heat.

'Fuck. Okay.' Her voice was all irritation and impatience. 'I'll be your old lady. Satisfied?'

No, I wasn't satisfied. And I wouldn't be until she
was mine in every way that counted. I always thought
she didn't feel that way about me, but there had been a
number of signs over the past couple of days that had
made me wonder…

A thrill shot down my spine. The kind of thrill I
hadn't felt for years.

'It'll do.' I made sure to let none of that show in my
voice, because frightening her off now would be a real
bad move.

'But it's not for real,' she insisted. 'We're just doing

this to protect Annie. Once Justin gets the message and backs off everything goes back to normal.'

Sure it would go back to normal.

Like hell.

Because I had a feeling that once I had Cat where I wanted her, wearing my property patch, I wasn't going to be able to let her go.

'It may not be for real to us.' I held her gaze. 'But it'll have to look real to convince Keep and the others.'

'Oh. But I thought...' She trailed off, frowning.

'He told me he wouldn't protect you as things stand. So I asked him outright if he would if you were mine, and he said yes.'

I paused, wanting to make sure she understood exactly what I was going to ask from her.

'If Justin makes a move and the club has to respond, it's going to put us at risk with the police. And Keep won't want to do that if he thinks you're faking it. In fact if he realises that, he's going to be pissed.'

He wouldn't just be pissed; he'd be furious. And I'd seen him furious. If I hadn't done my old man in, Keep would have, and it wasn't anything I wanted directed at either me or Cat.

Her frown deepened. 'So we have to pretend it's real? Is that what you're saying?'

'Yeah. He'll remember the conversation I had with him and he'll be suspicious, no question. We'll have to convince him we're the real deal.'

Cat dropped her attention to the pavement, studying it like it was the most fascinating thing she'd ever seen. And...was she *blushing*?

She'd done that a couple of nights earlier, avoiding my gaze, staring at anything other than me. Then there had been her weirdness about discussing that blow job and her furious denial that she'd been checking me out.

The electric thrill intensified.

I knew when a woman wanted me.

I knew when a woman wanted me and didn't want me to know.

Cat definitely didn't want me to know.

Fucking finally. After all these years...

Triumph surged like gas down a fuel line, lighting me right up.

She wanted me. She really did.

I couldn't help myself. I reached out, took her chin in my hand and tipped her head back, forcing her gaze to mine. Her eyes were dark and shocked, the green lost in the night.

'Is that going to be a problem?' I asked roughly.

She'd gone very still. Even in the dim light of the street I could see the fire in her cheeks and the quick beat of her pulse at the base of her throat.

The space between us had got thick, like the air before a thunderstorm.

I could hear my own heartbeat, loud and heavy in my head.

'I don't know...' She stopped. 'I mean, I don't...' She stopped again and cleared her throat. 'What exactly are you saying, Smoke?'

Her skin was soft under my fingers and I wanted to stroke her with my thumb, run it along the line of her lower lip, test how soft that felt, too.

'What do you think? We have to act like a real couple— know what I'm saying?'

She blinked, her attention dropping to my mouth. And staying there.

Holy fucking shit.

I was getting hard now, and my instinct was to push her against the brick wall and fuck us both into oblivion. But hard and fast up against a wall wasn't the way I wanted to do it—not with her and not after so many years.

No, I was going to take my time, make it last. Make her scream. Make her beg for me the way I would have begged for her if she'd only asked.

Maybe she could see that in my eyes, because she jerked her chin out of my grip, giving an abrupt, nervous-sounding laugh.

'That better not include sleeping with you, because you know that's not going to happen.' She was trying to make it sound like a joke and failing miserably.

For a second I debated asking her whether she was sure about that, but I kept my mouth shut. No point scaring her off before we'd even got started.

Still. I wasn't going to let this moment go—not yet.

'No,' I lied through my teeth. 'You're going to have to be comfortable with me touching you, though.'

She shifted on her feet, her Converses making scraping sounds on the pavement. Yeah, she was nervous, all right.

'Touching me how?'

I should have stopped right then. I should have let her go, turned around and taken her home.

But I didn't.

The devil had me in his grip and I wanted to keep pushing, to make her even more nervous. Because I'd been hanging out for her for years and now it was my turn to make her sweat.

I kept my posture loose and easy. Nothing threatening. Nothing that would scare her. But I held that green gaze of hers and let the hunger show.

'Come here and I'll show you.'

CHAPTER SEVEN

Cat

I STARED AT SMOKE, my heartbeat freakishly loud in my head.

Something was happening between us and it scared the shit out of me.

I knew as soon as I opened my big fat mouth and told him he didn't get a say about Annie that I'd crossed a line. That I'd hurt him and hurt him deeply.

I had no excuse except that I was frightened, and that when I got frightened I got angry.

Had *that* been the thing that had changed the atmosphere between us?

Or had it been the night I'd stormed into the clubhouse and seen Smoke getting head, with his hands in another woman's hair?

I didn't know. But maybe it didn't matter. Because right now it felt like I wasn't looking into my friend's eyes. It felt like I was looking into the eyes of a complete stranger.

And that stranger...

God, he was looking back at me like he wanted to eat me alive.

Like he looked at that woman in the hallway.

Shit.

Smoke made no move towards me. He simply stood there and put his hands in the pockets of his jeans, a relaxed kind of posture. But his gaze was black and there was fire in it—a heat I'd never imagined—not to mention challenge, too. Like he was daring me to do it.

I remembered that look. The first day I met him, after I'd watched him do tricks for a solid half-hour, he handed me his skateboard and dared me to try it. There had been many times after that when he'd pushed me to do something I didn't want to do or was scared of. Skateboarding. Riding his motorcycle. Drinking bourbon neat. Going to the school dance. Telling my mother she had to quit heroin or else I'd move out. Applying for law school. Leaving Justin…

Some of those things I'd ended up failing at, and some of them were among the best experiences of my life. But this challenge—this was different. This felt like it could threaten the very fabric of our friendship.

Seriously? You're acting like this is real and it's not. It's just pretend.

I drew in a shaky breath. Yeah, of course. Pretend. Which meant the way he was looking at me was pretend, too. He didn't really want me—just like I didn't really want him. Nothing would be threatened because we wouldn't actually be together. We'd just have to make it look like we were. And that was fine. I could do that.

Smoke wasn't wrong. No matter how much I didn't want to go anywhere near the Knights, this did seem to be our only option to protect Annie.

Plus, after what I said to him, I owed him.

'Okay.' I took a step away from the wall, getting closer to him. 'Show me, then.'

My voice sounded shaky and I couldn't seem to get my heart rate under control.

It was just Smoke. Only Smoke.

He stared down at me and I was suddenly aware of the height difference between us—something I'd only been vaguely aware of before. But it hit me now how much taller he was. How much broader. How much more powerful and muscular.

I wanted to make a joke about his workout regimen, yet I'd never felt less like laughing in my entire life.

'You'll have to come closer than that.'

His voice was quiet, with a dark, husky quality to it which was another thing I'd never noticed before.

I was looking at him like he was some stranger, but he wasn't. He was my friend.

I took another step towards him, trying to ignore my frantic heartbeat.

'That's better,' he said.

We were only inches apart now, and I could feel the heat of his body from where I stood. He was like the engine of his bike, running hot, and it was difficult to hold his gaze. The darkness of it was like a black lake I could fall into, drown in.

'So,' I said inanely, on edge and hyperaware, as if the slightest sound or sudden movement would cause me to jump sky-high. 'Are you going to?'

Smoke reached out and slid his arm around my waist, pulling me right up against his body. And everything I'd been going to say went straight out of my head.

I couldn't get enough air to breathe because he was hot. And hard. Everywhere. The arm around me was an iron band, holding me firmly where I was, and instinctively, I put up my hands and pressed my palms to the wall of his chest, trying to keep some distance between us.

But there was no distance to be had.

He was right there, up against every inch of me—my thighs, my hips, my stomach, my breasts. So fucking hot. So fucking hard. I could feel the flex and release of his muscles beneath my palms and I couldn't repress the shiver that went straight down my spine. The shiver of deep female appreciation for male strength. Insane when, after Justin, I knew what male strength could do to a woman.

I felt it, though. It made my mouth dry with want.

I was trembling and I couldn't stop. I felt like I was being slowly stripped down, taken apart like a gun or an engine, and all my pieces laid out so he could see how I was put together.

Don't be stupid. Pretend, remember?

Yeah. That's right. Pretend. Get a grip, Cat. Get a fucking grip.

I tilted my head back and looked up at him, because if this was a challenge, then I wanted to show him I could do it. I always wanted to show him I could do it.

The light behind him threw his face into shadow, but I could see his expression. It was taut, fierce, his gaze focusing on me with frightening intensity.

My heartbeat refused to slow down.

He lifted his other hand and, with careful deliberation, slid his fingers into my hair so they curved around my skull, cupping the back of my head in his palm. Then he curled his fingers up tight and I sucked in a startled breath as my hair was caught in his fist.

It didn't hurt, but I realised with a sudden crashing awareness that he was now holding me fast. That I couldn't pull away even if I wanted to.

And that he was going to kiss me.

'Smoke—' I began, to stop him…encourage him… I had no idea. I never got the chance.

His mouth was on mine before I knew what was happening.

I froze in shock, going rigid, my mind utterly blank.

Then heat erupted along the entire length of my body. *So* much heat. It was like one of those arc welders applied directly to my skin, lighting me up from the inside out.

Frightened for reasons I didn't understand, I pushed against his chest, wanting to get away, to put distance between us, between me and that all-consuming, terrifying heat.

But he didn't let me go. In fact the arm around my waist only tightened further, leaving me in no doubt about who was in charge of this. He was. In every way.

I shivered, feeling small and feminine, vulnerable and utterly at his mercy. Panic shifted inside me and something else—something that wasn't panic at all. Something that I very much feared was…excitement.

Then, before I could work out what the tangle of feelings were, slowly and deliberately Smoke continued to kiss me.

His lips were both hard and soft at the same time, brushing mine, a gentle tease. Then he ran his tongue along the seam of my lips, encouraging me to open and let him in.

I did and, oh, God, I tasted him. Raw, alcoholic, with a touch of sweetness like the kick of a really good bourbon. It made me tremble. Then his tongue slid into my mouth, exploring me, and I trembled even harder.

It had been so long since anyone had touched me like this, held me like this. So long since I'd been kissed. And now my best friend was kissing me and it felt like...

Jesus, it felt like a piece of a puzzle had clicked into place.

So wrong. This is your friend. This is pretend.

I tried to open my mouth to speak, to remind him or something—I didn't know. But he wouldn't let me do that either.

His fingers in my hair pulled tighter, urging my head further back, and his tongue pushed deeper into my mouth, the kiss turning hotter, wetter. More demanding. Taking all my words away and giving me heat and that sweet kick of bourbon instead, the raw, addictive taste of him.

My heartbeat was raging and I felt dizzy. Like I was drunk. On him. On this kiss. His heat was blinding and he was everywhere—his rock-hard chest against my aching breasts, his arms around me, holding me tight against him. His mouth was on mine, tasting me as I was tasting him. Kissing me as if he couldn't get enough. As if he wanted to eat me alive.

But, no. He couldn't want that. This was pretend, remember?

Yet my fingers curled into the warm cotton of his T-shirt, gripping on for dear life, and it was hard to hold on to that thought. He knew what he was doing and it was so good.

I couldn't help myself. I began to respond. Blindly

touching his tongue with mine, kissing him back, hungry for more of that terrifying heat. More of that kiss.

More of *him*.

My nipples hardened against his chest and there was a heavy, pulsing ache between my legs. My skin felt tight, like I wanted to burst right out of it.

Smoke growled—a low animal sound that vibrated through me—then he slid one large warm hand over the curve of my butt, pulling me harder against him. I nearly gasped as I felt the hard ridge of his cock press against the zipper of my jeans, causing jolts of intense pleasure as the zipper hit my clit.

I groaned, shifting my hips against his, helplessly chasing that friction. I felt like I'd been starved and he was tempting me with all my favourite foods, holding them out to me, giving me a taste, making me *so* fucking hungry...

Then suddenly his arms around me were gone; that hot, demanding mouth vanished, and I was stumbling forward, off balance, breathing fast and hard like I'd run ten marathons in a row.

I blinked, somehow finding my feet, trying like hell to get my breathing under control.

Smoke had pulled back and was standing there with his arms folded. The expression on his face was unreadable. He was watching me with a detached kind of focus. As if that whole kiss had merely been an experiment he wanted to see the effects of.

He hadn't felt it like I had, obviously.

Something fell away inside me—something that I refused to call disappointment. Because there was nothing disappointing about him not feeling that kiss. In fact it was reassuring. Clearly the intensity of it had been all in my head—a product of going too long without sex and nothing to do with chemistry at all.

Anyway, it made sense that he didn't feel it. Because he'd been pretending, too.

Sure, and maybe his cock had been pretending, as well.

Yeah, but guys got hard at the drop of a hat, didn't they? It wasn't me. It was merely the presence of a female body—that was all.

I sucked in a steadying breath, hiding my hardened nipples behind my folded arms, mirroring his posture.

'So?' I couldn't keep the husky edge from my voice. Dammit. 'That convincing enough for you?'

'It'll do.' His voice, in contrast, sounded completely normal, the asshole.

My heart raced and the heavy, nagging ache between my legs just wouldn't let up. Perhaps if I didn't think about it, it would go away.

'Good. So, how do we do this? I mean, do you simply tell them I'm your old lady and that's it? What?'

He hadn't moved. He was standing there like a statue, all tall and dark and radiating menace, not to mention a fair amount of distance.

He hadn't forgiven me for what I'd said to him.

If you break this friendship, it'll be your own fault. Don't forget you pretty much break everything you touch...

Panic turned over in my gut before I managed to shove the poisonous thought away. No, shit. Wherever that had come from, it was wrong. Sure, there were things in my life that hadn't gone to plan—but that was life, wasn't it? Shitty, shitty life.

I had Annie and I had Smoke—my two constants.

I wouldn't lose my daughter and I wouldn't break my friendship with Smoke. I just wouldn't.

'You going to do this, then?' he asked.

As if I had a choice.

'For Annie, yeah. I will.'

He gave a slow nod and I got the feeling that I'd agreed to something I didn't know anything about.

Panic gripped me again, but I forced it away. Being Smoke's pretend old lady... Really, how bad could it be?

A memory filtered through my consciousness of the night Annie had been taken, when I'd stormed through the Knights' clubhouse. All those men with all those women, having sex right out there in public, for everyone to see.

That was pretty bad.

'We...uh...we wouldn't have to do any...public stuff, would we?' I hated the quiver in my voice. 'Because, straight up, I'm *not* doing that.'

That distant look was still on Smoke's face, and it was like he was pulling away from me, even though he hadn't moved an inch. I wanted to reach out and grab his arm, pull him back.

'Don't worry.' Even his voice sounded remote. 'We wouldn't.'

'Okay, then.' I hesitated, then realised what I was doing.

I'd never hesitated in talking to Smoke before. Never, ever.

My throat closed. Things were different. Something had changed.

'Are we good?' I had to force myself to say it.

'Sure, kitten. We're good.'

But I didn't miss his own hesitation, and it slid like

a sliver of glass under my skin. I opened my mouth to
say something, but he'd already turned, jerking his head
in the direction of the kerb, where I saw the gleam of
chrome in the darkness. His Harley.

'Come on,' he said. 'I'll tell you the plan while I
take you home.'

CHAPTER EIGHT

Smoke

'SERIOUSLY? THAT'S YOUR PLAN?'

Tiger was stretched out on the couch opposite me, a beer in one hand, a joint in the other, and a woman in his lap. She was taking puffs on his joint and looking bored, obviously waiting until we'd finished talking so she could get on with the more important job of sucking his cock.

Unfortunately for her, we hadn't finished talking.

'Yeah, that's the plan.' I leaned back in my chair, picking at a hole in the cheap vinyl on the arm of it and trying not to let Tiger's sarcasm get to me. 'Something wrong with it?'

We were in the Knights' clubhouse, over by the corner near the pool table, where it was quieter and no one would overhear us. I'd just told him how I was going to save both Annie and Cat, and he'd told me what a fucking stupid idea it was.

'Uh…who's going to believe Cat's your old lady?' Tiger shook his head. 'Everyone knows she's your friend.'

'And everyone thinks I'm fucking her already.'

Which they did, since to them friendship between a man and a woman was apparently a goddamn unicorn. As in it didn't exist.

Tiger lifted his joint in salute. 'True.'

'So it's not exactly going to be a surprise.'

'Also true.' The woman sitting in his lap grabbed at his beer and he gave it to her. 'Though you taking an old lady might be.'

He wasn't wrong about that. I'd never wanted any permanent commitments and hadn't exactly kept it a big secret. Tiger was the same.

All I needed was my bike, my club, regular blow jobs and Cat. Sure, it would be great if Cat could provide the blow jobs, but you couldn't have everything.

That reminded me of the kiss a couple of nights ago and I shifted in my chair, trying not to think about it since every time I did I got harder than iron.

I'd been a prick to demand that of her, but I hadn't been sorry. Still wasn't. Because if nothing else ever happened between us, at least I'd have that kiss.

And, Christ, what a fucking kiss. I'd never had anything like it and I probably wouldn't have anything like it again.

She'd tasted exactly the way I'd dreamed, except better. Sweet, yet tart, too—like strawberries and really expensive dry champagne. Which was Cat all-up. It was also goddamn delicious and I wanted more.

Her body had felt soft and hot, and the moment the hard tips of her nipples had pressed against my chest, I'd wanted to eat her alive. Because that right there had been confirmation. She wanted me. She fucking *wanted* me.

Then she'd started to kiss me back and I'd nearly lost my mind.

I'd come *this* close to simply shoving her against the wall, pulling her jeans down and getting inside her as fast as I damn well could.

But I'd been good. I'd let her go, put her at a distance and made sure she knew it. Though if she'd tried to make like that kiss hadn't meant anything, like it was just some pretend shit between friends, I don't know what I would have done.

I'd never hurt Cat. But that didn't mean I was a good guy.

Anyway, I'd done what I'd intended. I'd put her off balance, shown her what there could be between us. And it was fucking incredible.

'Bro?' Tiger said, eyeing me. 'Have you *actually* been fucking her? 'Cause you've got that look on your face that—'

'No.' I cut him off. 'I'm not.'

At least not yet. And even if I was, it wasn't any of his business. It wasn't anyone's business except mine and Cat's.

'Sure, the brothers might be surprised I'm taking an old lady, but they'll just think we've finally acknowledged our feelings for each other or some such bullshit.'

'Yeah, I guess they will.' Tiger put his hand on the woman's thigh. 'What about if Justin goes after the kid? Think Keep'll definitely protect her?'

I scowled. 'He told me he would. He fucking better.'

'He's got shit going on with the police chief, though. He won't want to rock that particular boat.'

He wouldn't. Fucking politics. It was a necessary evil, though, especially with Keep trying to get us legit.

But that came with its own problems. Justin fucking
Grant being the main one—though hopefully Cat being
mine would make him think twice about coming for
Annie.

'So what are you going to do?' Tiger asked without
waiting for me to respond. 'Move her in here? Can't see
that happening, bro. She hates this place.'

'I know.'

I had my own plan about what I was going to do.
Sure, I could make her move in here with me, but the
clubhouse was no place for kids. Which left me with
only one option.

'Thought I'd move in with her.'

I hadn't talked to Cat about it and I wasn't going to
either. No point when she wasn't going to get a choice.
If we wanted it to look real, I was going to have to live
with her like a real couple would.

Tiger laughed. 'Oh, man, she's gonna *hate* that.'

He and Cat didn't get on. He thought she was up-
tight and a control freak, and she thought he was a dick.
Neither of them was wrong.

I shrugged. 'She'll have to suck it up.'

'Yeah, I'm sure she's going to have to do a lot of
sucking.' He gave another laugh and drained the rest
of his beer.

I said nothing to the stupid joke. Tiger had his demons,
and being a tool was all part of his don't-give-a-fuck deal.

'So when are you going to break the happy news?' He
slid his hand beneath the blonde's skirt and she shifted
around, flushing.

'The party this weekend. I'm bringing her along.'

Cat wouldn't like that either, since I knew she hated

club parties. Yet more stuff she was going to have to deal with.

The blonde nestled herself into the crook of Tiger's arm, her face pressed into his neck. It looked like things were only going to go downhill communicationwise, so I said, 'Catch you round, brother…' and got to my feet. 'I've got a few things to do before Saturday night.'

Like getting a property patch for my best friend.

'Can't wait for that.' Tiger grinned.

Then his gaze focused on someone behind me and his grin became wider.

'Good luck, man. Looks like you're gonna need it.'

I turned in time to see a curvy brunette coming across the room towards me, swinging her hips and giving me a sexy smile.

Fuck. It was Hannah. Blow Job Hannah.

She and I had an understanding. With her long dark hair and her delicate face it was easy to see—if you were looking—what I liked about her. She was my go-to girl when I couldn't get my goddamn best friend out of my head.

Probably I should have felt guilty about using her as a Cat stand-in, but I'd always figured it was better I do that than cut Cat out of my life completely. Yeah, I was a selfish fuck. I couldn't face the thought of doing that.

Cat was the one I turned to when Dad's fists had been harder than the walls he'd thrown me into. She patched me up, listened to me as I raged, and she gave me no judgement that night I ended those fucking hits forever.

Not seeing her ever again was not an option.

'Hey, Smoke.' Hannah sidled up. 'Been meaning to

catch up with you…see if you want to carry on where we left off, if you know what I mean.'

She gave her lips a surreptitious lick, to be sure I understood.

'I'm free now, if you are.'

Normally I would have been tempted—especially seeing as how it had been a week or so since that blow job and I'd been frustrated and on edge because of what was going on with Cat.

But that kiss had changed things, and the thought of letting off steam with Hannah didn't hold any attraction at all. Anyway, it seemed ridiculous to get Hannah to blow me when I could have the real thing in just a few short days.

If she lets you.

She'd let me. I'd make sure of it. And as for our friendship…it wouldn't be an issue—not when I wasn't planning on letting her go.

'Not now,' I said shortly, hoping she'd catch my drift.

She pouted and slid a hand over the front of my jeans, giving my dick a squeeze. 'Doesn't feel like "not now" to me.'

Because I'd been thinking of that fucking kiss, my dick was not uninterested in the thought of Hannah's mouth wrapped around it, the traitorous fuck.

'That's not for you.' I grabbed her hand and took it firmly away.

Her face fell and I thought I caught a look of genuine disappointment on it before she turned away, shrugging a shoulder.

'Your loss.'

Abruptly I felt like a tool. Some of the brothers didn't give a shit about club pussy. They didn't hurt the girls, but it wasn't like they cared either. The girls themselves knew what they were getting into when they hung around the clubhouse and slept with the brothers, but, hell, they had feelings like everyone else.

'Hannah,' I said, reaching out and grabbing her chin, turning her back to face me. 'It's not you, okay? I'm taking an old lady now, and that means I can't be doing that any more.'

And I wouldn't. Monogamy wasn't celebrated in the club, but I'd never been a fan of double standards. If Cat had to be faithful to me—and I sure as hell was going to expect that—then I'd do the same for her.

A rueful expression crossed her face. 'You're such a fucking problem. You're hot *and* a good guy, and there aren't many with that combination around here right now.'

I didn't know what to say, because she was wrong. I wasn't a good guy. Good guys didn't kill their fathers.

'I'm sorry, Hannah,' I said finally, and let her go.

Her eyes darkened. 'I'm sorry, too.'

Then she turned away before I had a chance to say anything more.

CHAPTER NINE

Cat

I'D JUST GOT Annie into the bath when my phone started buzzing with a call. I left her in the tub and stepped into the hallway, grabbing my phone from the pocket of my jeans and glancing down at the screen.

My heart sank right down into the bottom of my sneakers.

It was Justin.

Briefly I debated not answering it.

Tonight was the night of the party at the Knights' clubhouse—my debut with Smoke as a couple—and I had to bathe Annie and put her into bed before the sitter came, then get ready myself. I was in no mood to talk to my abusive ex.

Smoke had wanted us to go earlier in the evening, when there were apparently kids around, so Annie could go, too, but I didn't want that quite yet. I needed to check out the place first, before I brought her into it. He hadn't argued, had simply gone ahead and organised a sitter for her before I'd even broached the topic.

Now I wished I'd done what he said and gone early—then I wouldn't have to deal with this phone call.

Still, avoiding it would be cowardly, so I hit the answer button. 'What do you want?'

'Hey, don't be like that.'

Justin's smooth tones were warm and silky, like melted chocolate. To think I'd once loved his voice. What a lie it had been.

'I only want to talk.'

I gritted my teeth. 'What do you want to talk about?'

'Come on—don't play dumb. This is about Annie.'

'And?'

'What? Your boyfriend didn't tell you?'

'He's not my boyfriend,' I said reflexively. Then I realised what a mistake that was. Smoke *was* supposed to be my boyfriend. Crap.

'Yeah, like I ever believed that for a second.'

There was a bitterness I recognised in Justin's voice. He'd never liked my friendship with Smoke, and that had been the source of most of our arguments. Justin had wanted me to stop seeing him, but I'd refused. I wasn't cutting Smoke out of my life just because he couldn't handle the fact that my best friend was a guy.

'What do you want?'

I ran a hand through my hair, feeling exhausted. The past few days had been shitty. I'd been trying to find work to replace the shift at Lucky's, but hadn't managed to turn anything up, and rent was due at the end of the month—only a week away. I didn't have the money. Or at least I had the money for rent, but if we wanted to eat, then that might be problem.

'Like I said, this is about Annie. Thought I'd be a gentleman and let you know personally that I'm going to be suing for full custody in the next couple of weeks.'

He sounded so pleased with himself I wanted to punch him.

'Unless you agree to give me full custody yourself and then we can save all the messy court drama.'

My heart clenched tight. 'Why the hell would I do that?'

'Oh, come on, Cat.'

His voice had softened, taking on the warm and tender note that had once managed to reach inside me and undo all my defences. The note that told me I was cared for. That I was loved.

'Being a single mom is hard. You're working two jobs… You're tired every night. How is that good for Annie? Having such a tired mom all the time? And that apartment is a dump—not to mention dangerous. Mine is big, and there's security, and—hey, you know how much she loves swimming, right? I've even got a pool.'

His voice poured over me, smooth and rich, lulling me.

'If she was here, you wouldn't have to worry so much. You wouldn't have to work so hard all the time. The pressure would be off.'

I closed my eyes, horrified to find that if I wasn't careful I was going to burst into exhausted, emotional tears.

He was right. Being a single mom *was* hard and I worried *so* much. There was no break, no respite. Sometimes I wished I could just have ten minutes when I didn't have to worry about Annie and whether I had enough time for her. Whether I had enough money to feed and clothe her. Whether I could actually be the mother I wanted to be for her.

'It wouldn't mean you'd never see her,' he went on,

obviously knowing he'd hooked into my deepest fears. 'We'd work out a visitation schedule. Hell, you could even have her overnight a couple of times a week. Wouldn't that be better for you? You could actually spend time with her when you're not tired and worried and thinking about all the stuff you need to do.'

He knew me well. Knew what I was afraid of. Knew what I was desperate for. At first it had been so good to have someone know me like that. To love me the way I'd always wanted to be loved.

Then he'd shown me what a lie that was and how stupid I was to trust him. Just like he was lying to me now.

Never again.

I forced away the tears, swallowing back the lump in my throat. 'And if you get angry again, Justin?' I had to concentrate to make my voice sound strong and unaffected. 'What happens then? Will you hit Annie the way you hit me?'

There was a hard silence down the other end of the phone.

'That's not going to happen.' The warm note had vanished from his voice like it had never been there. 'I would never hit her.'

'The way you'd never hit me?'

'I've dealt with my anger issues,' he said calmly. 'Not that it would have ever happened if you'd done what I said and stopped screwing that friend of yours.'

Ah, *this* was the Justin I remembered. The asshole.

I said nothing—mainly because there was nothing to say. He wouldn't have listened anyway.

'Well? Last chance, Cat.'

'Why?' I asked suddenly. 'You never wanted her

before. You never wanted her in the first place. Why do you want her so desperately now?'

'Because she's *my* damn daughter, and I want what's mine. That's why.' He sounded impatient now. 'Are you going to give me full custody? If not, I'll see you in court.'

My jaw was tight, my heart burning with anger. 'No. I'll never give you full custody of her. Never, ever.'

He gave a snort of disgust. 'Stupid move, honey. Guess we'll have to do this the hard way, then.'

The call was disconnected abruptly.

Fuck. I didn't even have the satisfaction of hanging up on him.

My fingers were white around my phone, but I couldn't afford to give in to the urge to throw it at the wall because I literally couldn't afford to get a new one if it broke. I had to make do with shoving it hard into my pocket and cursing viciously.

It was difficult to go into the bathroom and continue bathing Annie like nothing had happened, but I managed it, and luckily she was too young to know that there was anything wrong.

Fifteen minutes later, all dry and dressed in clean pyjamas, Annie was ready for a bedtime story when the doorbell rang.

For a second I froze, the horrible thought of Justin coming over to take Annie away from me right now popping into my head. Then I remembered. The party. It would probably be either the sitter or Smoke.

Leaving her with a picture book, I crept into the hallway and went to the door and looked through the peephole.

Smoke was in the hall outside, in his jeans and cut, and he was literally the best thing I'd seen all day.

I undid the chain and pulled the door open, grinning stupidly. 'You're early. I wasn't expecting you till later.'

He didn't smile back the way he normally would have, and his gaze was fierce on mine. 'Thought I'd come and drop my stuff off.'

'What stuff?' Then I noticed the big duffel bag he had slung over one shoulder. 'What's that for?'

'What do you think? I'm moving in.'

My mouth dropped open—to say what, I had no idea. Because at that moment Annie came charging down the hallway, screaming, 'Smoke!' at the top of her lungs.

The fierce look vanished and a heartbreakingly beautiful smile crossed his face as he stepped past me.

'Hi, kiddo,' he said, opening his arms as Annie flung herself into them.

I shut the door and leaned against it, stunned by his announcement and by the fact that watching the pair of them together made my heart ache like someone had hit it with a large baseball bat.

He hadn't smiled at me. He'd saved it for Annie and that was okay. It really was. But seeing them together after that phone call with Justin hurt for reasons I didn't want to examine.

You should never have said that he wasn't her father.

No. I shouldn't have. Not when what was happening right in front of me proved what a lie that was.

Smoke had picked her up and was carrying her down the hallway.

'Can I read you a bedtime story, or do you want Mommy to do it?'

'You!' Annie said excitedly, then patted his shoulder. 'What's that big bag?'

'That? It's a unicorn. It was too big to carry, so I put it in the bag.'

Annie giggled, delighted. 'It is not!'

'No, it's not. It's only boring stuff like clothes.'

'I *like* clothes.'

'They're not for you, kiddo. They're for me. I'm going to be staying for a while.'

I watched Annie's face light up at this as they both disappeared through the doorway into her bedroom, belated shock moving slowly through my system.

Staying for a while...

He hadn't mentioned moving in when he'd told me his plan on the way back from Lucky's that night. All he'd said was that he wanted me to go to the party.

Panic turned over inside me and I didn't know why.

Ignoring it, I went down the hallway and into my bedroom, deciding I might as well get ready. He'd be with Annie awhile. I would wait to talk to him about this moving-in business once she was asleep.

Pulling open my closet, I grimaced at the lack of decent things to wear hanging in it. What the hell did you wear to a biker party anyway? The one and only party I'd been to had been the one where I'd caught Smoke getting that blow job, and none of the women at that party and been wearing anything at all.

God, I was *so* not going naked.

Pulling out a selection of things, I laid them on the bed, discarding my one and only little black dress as too dressy and the denim mini as too slutty. There was the plain black pencil skirt I wore to work at the call centre on occasion, but that seemed a little...boring.

This isn't a fashion show. You're not your mother.

I pulled a face, remembering my mom getting ready for the few parties Dad used to take her to. She'd always been so excited, thinking it meant something. Thinking that finally he was going to make her his old lady and everything would be different. She'd dress up in the few designer dresses she had left—the remains of her old, socialite life—and get herself looking beautiful.

But it never made any difference. And she always came home alone.

I always thought I'd never end up like her, and yet now here I was, a single mom, trying to find something to wear to a biker party. Even the fact that I was going as someone's old lady didn't change it—not when I wasn't a *real* old lady.

I was just like her. Struggling to make ends meet, to feed and clothe my kid. The only things I had going for me were that I wasn't an addict and I wasn't in love with a biker.

'Are you ready?'

I almost jumped at the sound of Smoke's deep voice coming from the doorway. He was leaning against the frame, his arms folded, the ink of his tats dark against his skin. That breathtaking smile he'd saved for my daughter was gone. The fiercely intense look was back again.

The same look he'd given me that night he'd kissed me.

I'd never felt shy around Smoke before, but I was now.

My mouth dry, I glanced down at the clothes on the bed. 'No, obviously, I'm not ready.'

I pushed aside the black dress, fiddling about with the black skinny jeans that were my favoured alternative.

'Annie must have gone down quickly.'

'She was tired. She said you were shouting at someone on the phone just before I arrived.'

Oh, shit. That kid had bat ears.

'Someone from work.'

I don't know why I didn't tell him about Justin. Maybe it was because Justin had made me feel so helpless and I didn't want Smoke to know how badly affected I was.

'Bullshit. Annie said you were talking about her.'

Busted.

I let out a breath, smoothing the fabric on the bed. 'It was Justin. He was trying to get me to give him sole custody voluntarily.'

I didn't even know Smoke had moved until I felt heat beside me and a powerful hand had my jaw in its grip, turning my face to his.

Black eyes pinned me. 'And you said what?'

'What do you think? Of course I said no.'

But he must have heard the catch in my voice because that fierce look suddenly softened. 'What else did he say, Cat?'

His thumb brushed absently along the line of my jaw, striking sparks along every nerve ending I had. I tried not to notice, tried not to shiver.

'He made like it would be a good thing.' My voice thickened. 'He told me it would be better for Annie if she didn't have a mom who was working all the time and who was so tired. Who had no time for her kid because she was always worrying. And he said how his apartment was safe, and he has a pool, and you know how much she likes swimming—'

I broke off, my eyes prickling, and tried to pull away again, not wanting Smoke to see how much Justin's words had slipped beneath my skin. How much they'd made me doubt myself.

But Smoke didn't let me go. 'There's no better place for Annie than with you,' he said with quiet emphasis. 'She doesn't need a fucking pool. All she needs is love, and you do that better than anyone.'

My heart swelled up tight in my chest. 'Sometimes I can't help thinking that maybe she'd be better off with him. He has money and—'

'Quiet,' Smoke interrupted, with so much authority I fell silent. 'That prick's got nothing Annie needs. If he was any kind of decent father, he would be in her life, but he's not. And if he was any kind of decent man, he wouldn't have fucking touched you in the first place. But he did. Which makes him and his opinions worth *shit*.'

I opened my mouth to tell him how much I'd needed to hear that that, but he put his thumb across my lips and pressed down lightly, silencing me.

'Don't worry, kitten,' he went on softly. 'You don't need to worry—especially not about money. I'm here now, and I'll deal with it.'

I had issues with that, but for some reason my brain wouldn't work. I couldn't repress the helpless shiver that chased over my skin at his touch either.

A black flame leapt in his eyes, hot and dark, and for a second I had the mad urge to open my mouth and suck on his thumb. Bite it.

Maybe he saw that, too, because I swore I caught the flicker of a feral kind of smile on his beautiful mouth.

'Black pencil skirt. Green blouse. Black stilettos. Stockings.' His hand fell away, releasing me. 'Now, go get ready. The sitter will be here any minute.'

CHAPTER TEN

Smoke

THE PARTY WAS already underway by the time Cat and I got to the clubhouse. We were hosting The Demon's Share brothers—a smaller club from down south who were allies—and us Knights always liked to put on a good show.

The rides were parked outside—a massive line of them, chrome gleaming under the streetlights—and the prospects assigned to guard them were hanging out by the doorway, smoking and drinking and flirting with a bunch of girls who were trying to get in.

I helped Cat off my bike, unable to keep my eyes off her as she smoothed down the skirt that had got rucked up on the ride over.

She'd put on exactly what I told her to and she looked so fucking *hot*—exactly as I'd pictured her. The pencil skirt hugged her ass like a greedy pair of hands, and the soft green blouse was transparent enough to see the lacy black bra she wore underneath it. Plus, it was nearly the same colour as her eyes.

The effect was like a classy, sexy secretary. She'd

even done her hair in a loose bun that I wanted to pull the pins out of and run my fingers through.

All she was missing was my property patch on her back.

Well, I'd fix that once we were inside. My plan was to take her in, claim her in front of all the brothers so no one could be in any doubt, and when she came out again, she'd be my old lady.

My property.

A deep satisfaction sat in my gut, along with a desire so strong it was like a kick to the head.

Tonight I'd make her mine.

Finished with smoothing herself, she flicked a nervous glance at the doorway. Nervous was okay, though. Nervous was better than the weariness I'd seen in her face earlier, when she was standing by her bed looking at her clothes. Better than the terrible doubt when she'd told me what that asshole Justin had said to her.

He was a bastard for hooking into her doubts and using them against her, and I wanted to kill the guy with my bare hands. Hell, when he came for Annie with that custody order, maybe I'd even get the chance.

'It'll be okay,' I said to reassure her. 'It's not like your dad's club, remember?'

The Knights looked after their own way better than her old man's club had. And even if they didn't, *I* sure as hell did.

'Thanks, *Dane*,' she said tartly, pissed off that I'd picked up on her nervousness. 'I'll take that under advisement.'

I almost grinned. 'You want to be careful, Cat. I might call you *kitten* in there, and then you'll be stuck with it for life. The brothers like a nickname.'

She rolled her eyes, but her mouth curved, and for a second, we were almost friends again. Then I remembered the way that mouth had tasted, and all the things I wanted to make it do, and I knew that it couldn't happen.

Because I didn't want friendship—not from her.

Friendship wasn't enough any more.

Reaching out, I grabbed her hand, lacing her fingers through mine. 'Ready?'

'As I'll ever be, I guess.'

We walked up to the entrance, ignoring the wide-eyed stares of the girls still trying to get in. The prospects gave me a chin jerk as we approached, stepping aside. As we went past them I could see them give Cat appreciative glances, no doubt noting the fact that she didn't have a property patch on her back.

I gave the little fucks my enforcer stare and they quickly looked away.

Damn straight.

There were a lot of people milling around—Knights and more than a few Demons. Some of them called my name, but I didn't stop, heading down the corridor that led out to the back of the building where the courtyard was.

That tended to be where the action was whenever there was a party, which meant Keep would be there. And it was him I wanted to see first of all. I needed him to know what I was going to do, because it was only polite to inform my president. Especially if he was going to give me shit about it.

Then I was planning to get the vest with the property patch on it and make Cat put it on in front of the whole club, so there would be no doubt about whose she was. So everyone would know she was fucking *mine*.

We went through the doors at the end of the hallway and outside into the courtyard, and sure enough a bonfire was blazing in the middle of the space.

There were plenty of people milling around, talking and drinking, some dancing to the music that was blaring from the outdoor speaker system. The smell of cigarettes and weed was in the air, combining with the scent of burning wood from the fire, reminding me of what I loved about the club so much.

It was home. It was friendship. It was having people at your back who you could trust with your life. It was being part of a family. It was everything I'd never had as a kid.

And now it would be Cat, too.

I led her through the crowds, spotting Keep's tall figure over by the fire. He was talking to Big Red, the VP, and Chase, the president of Demon's Share.

Some of the brothers were beginning to stare at us, nudging each other and grinning.

'Fuckin' told ya,' someone muttered as we went by.

I ignored all of them, catching Keep's eye as we approached, tightening my fingers around Cat's.

His brows rose, his gaze flicking to Cat, then back at me. 'What the fuck is this?'

I could feel Cat stiffen beside me, so I ran my thumb over the back of her hand in reassurance. Keep had met Cat a couple of times before but only in passing.

'It's exactly what you think it is,' I said.

Keep didn't take his eyes off me. 'Why don't you get Leanne to show Cat where to find a drink, Red? I need to talk to Smoke here for a second.'

Leanne was Red's old lady, and the fact that Keep had asked her to look after Cat was a sign he thought she was more than a casual fuck. But the look on his face was *not* friendly. Luckily it was directed at me, and I could handle it.

He might be my president, and my uncle, but he wasn't going to tell me who I could and couldn't have as my property. He mightn't like it, but in this case he was going to have to suck it up.

'Smoke—' Cat began, obviously not liking where this was going.

'It's okay.' I turned to meet her uncertain green eyes and cupped her cheek in my palm, blatantly taking advantage of our pretence to touch her. Her skin was so soft and so warm, and I allowed myself to enjoy the feel of it. 'I'll come find you in a second.'

I could tell she didn't want to go, but after a gesture from Red brought Leanne over, she allowed herself to be led off.

'Mind telling me why she's here?' Keep asked in the quiet voice he only used when someone was in deep shit.

Everyone else suddenly found other things to do, melting away into the rest of the crowd, leaving Keep and me alone.

I stared back, holding my ground. I knew he was going to be pissed, but I wasn't budging when it came to Cat and Annie's safety. I'd do anything I could to make sure the pair of them stayed where they belonged. *With me.*

'I think you know why she's here,' I said flatly. 'Going to make her my old lady.'

Keep's expression didn't change. He was a man who kept his feelings close to his vest. A family trait, that.

'This got something to do with what we talked about last week?'

No point in denying it. 'Yeah.'

His eyes had got cold. 'So you're willing to put at risk everything we worked for—everything *I* worked for—to save your friend?'

He said it casually, like it was no big deal. Generally that was a sign that it was a huge fucking deal.

I knew that. I knew what bringing Cat here would mean.

'It's not just her. It's the kid, Keep. It's Annie. She's six years old. You really want her to go back to her violent old man?'

It was a low blow that went deeper than just Annie and Cat, and Keep knew it.

I was talking about my dad. About how everyone had known he was handy with fists, that he knocked me and Mom around, and yet no one had done anything. Not until the day he hit Mom once too hard and she went into the hospital and never come out again.

It was only then that someone tried to do something. Me.

'Or is it not our business?' I stared hard at him. 'Not our fucking problem?'

He shifted, folded his arms, and I knew that I'd got to him.

'Jesus, Smoke. You're just playing pretend with her—I can see that. I've never believed she was anything more than your friend, no matter what the others said.'

I took a couple of steps until I was right in front of him, looking him right in the eye. It was a direct challenge, but sometimes that was the best way to handle things with Keep. The truth didn't hurt either.

'She's mine,' I said. 'She always has been, and she always will be.'

Keep's blue stare flickered. 'And if she puts the Knights at risk because of her fucking ex? Will you be saying the same thing then?'

'You can talk to the police chief. You can get him to call his motherfucking son off.'

'Yeah, and that'll damage the relationship we have with him—you know that.'

'We can handle it.' Hell, we'd handled every other challenge that had been thrown at us over the years. We could handle this, too. 'Unless, of course, you think we're not strong enough.'

Keep gave a short laugh. 'You're trouble, boy. I knew you would be.'

I didn't argue, and I didn't look away. 'I'm going to take her, Keep. Whether you like it or not.'

My uncle stared at me for a long, uncomfortable minute. 'For the record, I don't like it, and I'm not happy about it. And if this all goes to shit because of it, we'll all know where the blame lies. Understand?'

'Sure. I understand.'

He was silent, the look on his face unreadable. 'This is one favour you're going to owe me. Are we clear?'

I didn't like the sound of that, but what else could I do but agree? 'Yeah, crystal.'

Keep let out a breath. 'Okay, then, you claim her. But I'll need the pair of you to fuck off out of my sight for a couple of days.'

Like that was going to be a problem. If everything

went the way I wanted it to, Cat and I wouldn't come up for air for at least a week.

But first things first.

There was a patch I needed to get.

CHAPTER ELEVEN

Cat

I DIDN'T MUCH like being shunted off with Leanne. It felt too much like being dismissed, leaving the men to talk about the important stuff while the women weren't to worry their pretty little heads, et cetera.

But Leanne was very up-front about that kind of behaviour.

'It's all bullshit,' she said as she handed me a beer from the cooler that sat under a nearby table. 'The brothers wave their dicks around like that all the time.' She smirked. 'Sometimes literally. Just ignore it. I do.'

'I'll keep that in mind.'

I sipped my beer, my attention on the two men by the bonfire.

Keep, the Knights' president, was about as tall as Smoke, but built on an even more massive frame. He had shoulders like a pro wrestler's and biceps that would have put Superman to shame. There was an air of contained violence about him, a menace that had me shivering inside. He was a good-looking guy, though. Black hair and blue eyes and a charisma that was almost palpable. I knew he was Smoke's uncle and I could kind of see the resemblance.

I didn't like that air of violence, though. It reminded me too much of people like Smoke's asshole of a father. Of Justin. Men who couldn't handle themselves and took to beating people up instead.

Smoke was standing right in front of him, looking him right in the eye, and I felt a sharp spike of trepidation. God, was he putting himself and his membership of the Knights on the line for me and Annie? It made me feel uncomfortable, made me want to protest. I knew what the Knights meant to him, and even though I didn't like them I respected the fact that they were important to him. I wouldn't want him leaving because of me.

Leanne had opened her mouth to say something when the VP, Big Red—black bearded and green eyed—came up behind her, putting his arms around her and bending to whisper something in her ear. She laughed and then shrieked as he started dragging her off towards the entrance of the clubhouse.

They disappeared inside and I was conscious of standing beside the table on my own, in a crowd full of leather-clad, tattooed bikers. There seemed to be a lot more than there was before, and the women around were of the short-skirt, tight-top kind.

By the fire, Smoke turned on his heel and strode off towards the clubhouse. Keep's gaze followed him.

God, I hoped nothing bad had gone down.

There was a high-pitched giggle not far from me as one of the girls was pulled into the arms of a biker, his hand pushing down under her top.

Great. So the sex games were already starting.

'Hey, pretty.'

There were hands on my hips, pulling me back against a wall of leather before I had a chance to protest.

'Looks like things are heating up. You need cooling down?'

The voice was unfamiliar. A hand slid up and cupped my breast.

'No. Fuck off.' I jerked myself away and turned around.

A massive guy with a greasy black beard stood behind me, glowering at me. He wasn't a Knight from the look of his cut. He was from The Demon's Share.

'That's no way to treat a brother, bitch,' he said belligerently. 'You ain't got no patch on your back, so how about you fucking show me some respect?'

This was bad. I took a shaky breath, trying not to panic. 'I'm Smoke's,' I said, with as much calm as I could. 'And he'll be fucking pissed you laid a hand on me.'

'Uh-huh. But, like I said, I don't see a patch on your back, which means—'

'Which means she's fucking Smoke's.'

Tiger's tall, muscled figure was suddenly between me and the bearded shithead.

'So how about you go find someone else to play with?

The other man grunted and with one last evil look at me turned and pushed his way into the crowd.

Relief left me feeling unsteady, so I leaned surreptitiously against the table, trying not to show it. 'Thanks, Tiger,' I muttered.

He turned, his weird golden eyes glinting in the firelight. 'What the fuck's Smoke doing leaving you here alone?'

'I had Leanne with me, but Big Red took her away. Smoke just went into the clubhouse.'

'Huh. Fucking idiot.' Tiger raised the beer he was holding and took a long swallow, his gaze never leaving mine. It was guarded, suspicious. 'I'd better stay with you, then. Make sure no other fucker tries to take a shot at you.'

I wanted to tell him he didn't need to, that I could take care of myself, but clearly that would be playing the 'stupid' card one too many times. So I said nothing, turning away and gazing at the gathered crowd of bikers as they whooped and hollered around the fire.

There were a couple of live-sex shows happening already and I could feel my face flaming.

I looked away, my heart hammering, wishing I was anywhere but here.

Tiger said nothing, guarding me silently, warning anyone who came near with a hard stare.

It was uncomfortable and awkward, and I was on the point of saying I'd go inside and find Smoke myself when an arm snaked around my waist, drawing me up against hard muscle and heat. But this time it was familiar and I leaned into it with relief before I could stop myself.

'You okay, kitten?'

Smoke's deep voice was in my ear.

'Yes.'

I wanted to turn and lay my head on his chest, relax for a second. But I didn't.

'I'm fine.'

'You shouldn't have left her alone, man.' Tiger was scowling. 'Already had Bear trying to stake a claim.'

Smoke's arm tightened around me and I was acutely

conscious of the feel of him against my back. Heat and strength and the dark, earthy scent of a forest.

'Leanne was supposed to be looking after her.'

'Red decided he had other plans for Leanne,' Tiger muttered.

'I'm fine,' I repeated, annoyed at being talked about like I wasn't there and irritated by the relief I felt at Smoke's return. 'Tiger looked out for me.'

Surprise flashed in Tiger's eyes, as if he wasn't expecting that. Okay, so I didn't much like the guy, but I appreciated him being there.

'Thanks, bro,' Smoke said. 'I owe you.'

'Yeah, well, you'd better hurry this show along.' Tiger jerked his head towards the fire. 'I got better things to do than guard women.'

Smoke released me, then took my hand. 'Come on. Time we introduced you to the club.'

My gut twisted. I didn't know what I expected, but clearly whatever it was that Smoke was going to do he was going to do it in front of everyone.

I tried to calm myself down as he led me over to the bonfire. People were turning to look at us and I felt self-conscious in my pencil skirt and stiletto heels. No other woman was wearing clothes like that and I felt overdressed. As we got closer to the fire, I began to feel hot and panicky.

'Hey, assholes!'

Keep's deep voice cut through the noise like a sharp knife through leather. He was standing on the other side of the fire and had obviously seen us coming.

'Shut the fuck up for a second! Smoke's got something to say.'

Surprisingly, everyone quieted, turning to look at

where Smoke and I stood. His fingers, laced through mine, were warm, his grip firm, and I had a strange urge to pull away and start running. Get away.

'To all those fuckers who've taken bets on whether Cat and I are together!' Smoke shouted, his voice husky, gritty, with a thread of what sounded like triumph winding through it. 'It's time to either collect what you're owed or pay up.'

He lifted his other hand and I saw he was holding something in it. A black leather vest, like the cut he wore. On the back was a patch that read Property of Smoke, Knights of Ruin MC.

People cheered. Some of them shouted encouragement and punched their fists into the sky. Others called out cheerful yet filthy curses.

The firelight leapt across Smoke's face as he looked at me, the flickering shadows making him a stranger. His eyes were as dark as the night sky above our heads and he was smiling. But it wasn't the amused, friendly smiles I was used to. This was different. It was hungry… feral. A predator's smile.

He held up the vest between his hands and it was obvious what he wanted me to do.

People were shouting and cheering as I walked over to him, the ground feeling unsteady under my feet. My heartbeat was loud in my head, and despite the beer I'd had, my mouth was dry.

This was insane. It was pretend. Why the hell was I feeling so weird about it?

I turned when I got to Smoke, giving him my back while I held my arms out. He put the vest on me, the leather hot and heavy against my spine.

The brothers were shouting and cheering, raising

their beer bottles or whatever else they were drinking into the sky.

I couldn't get a breath. The whole situation was freaking me out. This was what Mom had wanted—what she'd been desperate for Dad to give her—and now I had it. Now I was part of a club, even though it was the last thing in the world I wanted.

Smoke's hands settled on my shoulders and he turned me around. The stranger's smile had gone. Now he simply looked intense, the way he'd looked right before he'd kissed me outside Lucky's.

My pulse began to go crazy as he lifted a hand, sliding his fingers around the back of my head, drawing me close. I wanted to push at him, keep the distance between us, because I wasn't ready for this. But his mouth was on mine before I had a chance to do anything about it.

It was another hot, possessive kiss that had my toes curling in my stilettos. And he wasn't slow this time, or coaxing. His tongue pushed deep into my mouth, demanding and hungry, and all I could do was let him take whatever he wanted.

People were shouting all around us and then the kiss was over. Smoke was lifting his head. His grin was pure triumph, pure satisfaction—almost the same as the grin that had lit his face the day he'd first brought his Harley home.

The possessive hand at the back of my head dropped to my waist, curling around me as he brought me close to his side.

I swallowed and muttered, 'Now what?'

People were starting to approach us, guys slapping

Smoke on the back and congratulating him, calling him a sneaky motherfucker and then grinning at me.

'Now we enjoy the party,' he said, his arm like an iron bar around me.

'Can't I just go home?'

'No.' There was no arguing with that tone. 'You want to make this look real? We have to make it look real.' He glanced down at me, his black eyes glittering in the firelight. 'Unless you want to go to my bedroom here?'

My stomach lurched at the same time as an electric thrill shot through me. He was joking, of course. He had to be, didn't he?

I looked away, back at the crowds. 'Uh…no, I'm fine.'

The music thumped and the party started to get more raucous, as if Smoke's announcement had been some kind of signal to finally go wild.

Tiger had joined a group by the fire, all gathered around a short, curvy brunette in a tiny skirt and tank top who was grinding away to the music. As I watched, the brunette turned to Tiger and put her arms around his neck, her hips still grinding, giving him what was basically a vertical lap dance.

She looked familiar to me for some reason.

Tiger bent his head, whispering something in her ear, and she tipped her head back, laughing. Then she dropped to her knees in front of him and reached for his zipper.

Okay, *now* I recognised her. It was the woman I'd seen giving Smoke a blow job in the hallway.

Beside me Smoke was easy, relaxed, and when I flicked a glance at him I saw he was watching the show the woman and Tiger were putting on. I found myself studying him for signs that he minded what was happening in front of us, but there was no jealousy in his face whatsoever.

'It was just a blow job, Cat,' he said, without looking at me, like he knew exactly what I was thinking. 'It didn't mean anything.'

'I wasn't… I mean, I didn't…' I couldn't finish.

He glanced down at me. 'Are you jealous?'

I could feel my cheeks heat. 'No, don't be stupid.'

I turned back to the show by the fire. I didn't want to watch what was going on in front of us—I really didn't. Yet something in me wouldn't let me look away as the woman began to give Tiger a blow job right in front of everyone.

Smoke's hand moved, sliding up to cup my breast.

I went still, the breath catching in my throat.

My blouse was very thin, and his hand felt like one of the coals from the fire, burning right through the material. Then his thumb brushed over my nipple. Electricity shot through me and I nearly gasped aloud. He began to circle my painfully hard nipple through my blouse slowly, lightly, and I shuddered before I could stop myself.

'What are you doing?' I asked thickly.

He didn't turn his head, his attention still on the show that was being performed in front of us. 'Making it look real.'

My mouth was dry and I couldn't hear anything else through the sound of my heartbeat. There was a deep, aching pulse between my thighs, an intense pressure.

Tiger drained his beer and tossed the bottle away, so he could put both hands in the woman's hair, moving his hips faster.

112   RUINED

Don't, I wanted to say to Smoke. *Please don't.*

I didn't know why I didn't. Because this was wrong—this shouldn't be happening. He shouldn't be touching me and I shouldn't be getting worked up about it.

But he was. His thumb was moving in slow, aching circles around my nipple, making me tremble, making it hard to breathe.

This wasn't making it look real. No one could see his hand, so what the hell was he doing?

A blind, unreasoning panic squeezed my chest tight, and before I knew what I was doing, I'd jerked away from him, turning and shouldering my way through the crowd, heading towards the clubhouse. Someone called my name but I ignored them.

I had no idea where I was going or why. I only knew I had to get away from what was happening in front of me, away from the woman and Tiger, and most of all away from Smoke. From the intense, hungry feeling that had wrapped its hands around my throat and refused to let go.

There were crowds inside the corridors of the clubhouse, but I didn't meet anyone's eyes, walking blindly, not looking where I was going. I didn't even have a direction. I only wanted to get away, find somewhere I could be alone and figure out what was happening to me.

I didn't realise I'd gone through the main set of clubrooms and into the back of the clubhouse, where all the bedrooms and other offices were, until the dim lighting and the lack of people brought me to a stop. There were lots of doors in the hallway and the sound of people talking behind them—other sounds, too, of pleasure.

The place was familiar. And I knew why.

'There's a reason you came here,' a voice said from behind me, deep and dark and full of rough heat. 'Isn't there, Cat?'

Smoke. He'd followed me.

I sucked in a ragged breath, my legs trembling. No, I had no idea why I'd come here—to the place where I'd found him getting a blow job from that woman. I should have gone out to the front, called a taxi and gone home.

But I hadn't.

His footsteps sounded behind me and I tensed, but he walked past me, going down the hall a little way. Then he stopped and turned, leaning back against the wall, looking straight at me. His hands were in his pockets. There was nothing threatening in his stance. Yet I felt like he'd pinned me where I stood all the same.

He'd brought the heat of the bonfire inside with him and the flames were flickering in his eyes.

'Come here,' he ordered softly.

I couldn't tell myself I didn't know what was happening between us any more. I couldn't tell myself this was only pretend. I couldn't tell myself I didn't want it more than I wanted my next breath either.

I'd run from him, but I hadn't run in the direction I should have. I'd run here.

He was right—there was a reason for that.

My feet were moving before I even knew what I was doing. I was walking towards him as if he had control of me, as if he was reeling me in like a fish on the end of a line. I stopped in front of him, my breath coming hard and fast in time with my hammering pulse.

He looked calm and relaxed, leaning back against the wall. Except for his eyes. They burned so bright.

'On your knees.'

Again the order was soft, yet there was no denying the authority of it. I found myself doing exactly what he said, dropping to my knees in front of him.

It seemed like years since the night I'd come here and found him getting blown by that woman. When my mind, the traitor, had wondered what it would be like to be that woman.

Now I was going to find out.

The thought made me dizzy.

He lowered one hand and slid his fingers along my jaw. I shivered.

'You know what to do, kitten.'

I swallowed and reached to undo the top button of his jeans. My hands were shaking, but somehow I managed it. He put his own hand over mine, directing my fingers, helping me draw the zipper down.

Oh, Jesus. I was going to do this right here, in the hallway, where anyone could find us. Just like I'd found him a week ago. Maybe I was drunk… Maybe I was stoned. Maybe I was insane.

Maybe this is just what you've always wanted…

His fly was undone now, and I could see his cock pressing against the black cotton of his boxers. He was hard.

I felt weirdly disconnected from myself as he guided my hand inside his jeans, using his free hand to pull down the cotton. Then my fingers were sliding over his cock, lifting him out, and he was long and thick and hard. God, *so* hard.

Someone was panting. It was me.

I took him in my fist. His skin was hot and smooth and it felt like velvet. I couldn't remember the last time I'd wanted to taste something so badly in all my life.

He guided my fingers up the length of him, and half of me was already a little insane with desire. The other half was horrified at what I was doing. His hand tightened around mine, making me squeeze him, but it was my thumb that rubbed over the slick head. The feel of him was so good.

Dimly something screamed at me that this was *Smoke*, my best friend, and that sucking your best friend's dick was pretty much guaranteed to ruin a perfectly good friendship. But I couldn't seem to think about why that was.

'Look at me.' His voice had deepened, become thick and hoarse.

I obeyed, letting the darkness and the flames in his eyes wash over me, consume me.

'Suck me, Cat,' he ordered.

So I leaned in, inhaling the musky, woody scent that was all Smoke, and I opened my mouth, touched my tongue to the head of his cock, licking at him delicately. The salty flavour of him burst on my tongue and I heard the sudden harsh intake of his breath.

'No. Put my cock in your mouth.' There was a desperate edge to his words now. 'Fucking *do* it, kitten.

I didn't hesitate, responding to him on the most basic level, taking him in as deep as I could, the size of him stretching my mouth wide, letting him nudge the back of my throat.

He groaned. The sound was a caress, like he'd run his hand right the way down my naked body. It was the most unbelievably erotic thing I'd ever heard and I wanted more of it.

I gripped his cock harder, squeezing as I sucked him,

using the pressure, using my tongue, taking him even deeper.

'Cat...'

The sound of my name was threaded through with hunger. He took his hands out of his pockets and pushed his fingers into my hair, holding on so tight that prickles of pain erupted all over my scalp. Hairpins fell onto the floor as the weight of my hair fell out of its loose bun and slowly down my back. I didn't care.

He was holding me the way he'd been holding that woman, directing me the way he'd directed her. And the look in his eyes was the same—intense and so hungry I nearly caught fire.

'You know...who I was...thinking about...when you saw me with her?'

He knew what I was thinking about. Of course he did.

'You, kitten. I was thinking about...you...'

Shock coursed through me.

Me. He'd been thinking about *me*.

That meant something—something I wasn't prepared to face just yet. So I ignored it. I concentrated instead on what I was doing: sucking him deep, pumping him with my fist, turning him inside out the way he'd been doing to me for the past week. Watching him as he groaned again, his head tipping back, exposing the strong muscles of his throat.

'Oh, fuck... Cat...'

The harsh edge in his voice was the sexiest thing I'd ever heard in my life. I could feel his hands in my hair trembling.

I was doing this to him. This strong, immovable man. *I* was making him shake. *I* was making him desperate.

I couldn't take my eyes off him. Lines of agonised pleasure were carved into his familiar, beautiful face, and the sounds that were coming from him—harsh and deep, ragged gasps of breath—made the ache between my thighs even worse.

I didn't want this to end. Because in that moment I felt more powerful than I ever had in my entire life.

I thought being on your knees meant you were weak, that you were beaten, with your eyes swelling shut and the sick, bitter taste of defeat in your mouth.

Not here. Not now. Not with Smoke.

No, Smoke made me feel like there was more to my power than I'd ever dreamed possible. But that was what he always did. He made me feel powerful even when I'd thought I wasn't.

His hands were tightening on my head and he began to direct my movements, flexing his hips, thrusting faster, harder, and I let him do it—let him take control of me.

'Fucking look at me, Cat,' he whispered roughly as I let my lashes fall shut. 'I want your eyes up here.'

So I looked at him, meeting the ferocious blackness in his gaze, holding it.

This is going to change everything. Nothing will be the same again.

I ignored that unwelcome thought and lost myself in my best friend's dark eyes, watching as the climax hit him, as his head was thrown back as he called my name, raw and harsh, his fingers in my hair a sweet agony. As he came down the back of my throat and I swallowed everything he gave me.

There was silence afterwards, broken only by the ragged sounds of his breathing and the thunder of my

own heartbeat. I didn't want to think about anything—
not what was going to happen later, or what it meant
for our friendship. What it would change and what it
would break.

Because something always got broken when lines
were crossed. Always.

His hold in my hair eased as he withdrew from my
mouth, and I rested my cheek against the hot skin of
his taut stomach and closed my eyes, feeling the flex
and release of hard muscle in time with his breathing.

I was aching, the pulse between my thighs heavy
and insistent, but I didn't want to move. I wanted to
stay here, in this peaceful moment, where it was just
him and me and silence. Where we didn't have to talk
or angst about the choices we'd made… Where the only
thing that mattered was the feel of his fingers in my
hair, gently massaging my scalp.

But of course it didn't last.

He was still semihard and getting harder with every
second. Then the gentle hands in my hair weren't so
gentle any more as he pulled me to my feet.

I looked up at him, abruptly panicking about what
this would mean for our friendship, opening my mouth
to tell him that we had to put this behind us, that we had
to pretend it hadn't happened. Yet before I could say
anything he bent his head and his lips were on mine,
the kiss forcing my head back, forcing my mouth to
open for him.

The demand in his kiss made me tremble—because
there was no resisting him, no holding out or holding
back. He took everything. His tongue was pushing inside,
sliding along mine, exploring me, and he must have tasted

himself because he growled all of a sudden, his fingers tightening around my upper arms.

Then we were moving as he walked me backwards down a short, dark, dead-end corridor. There was one door to the left, a blank wall to the right, and he pushed me into the corner where the blank wall met the end of the corridor. His hands were pressed to the wall on either side of my head, his big, lean body caging me there while he kissed me, deep and wet, with total and absolute demand.

The scent of him—so familiar and yet now so heavy with the musk of male arousal—was the most erotic thing in the entire goddamn universe. And the heat of him, so agonisingly close to me, was making me crazy.

Yet I was shaking. Because some part of me knew what was going to happen next and I was terrified. It would be a step we couldn't come back from. I knew that deep in my soul.

Like that blow job hasn't changed things already?

Of course it had. But this…this was different. It was one thing to turn him inside out, make him come. It was quite another to give him the same power over me.

His hands dropped from the wall to grip the fabric of my skirt, pulling it up higher and higher. My breathing was fast and I felt dizzy, as if I didn't have enough air. I reached for his hands to push them away, but he was too strong, too insistent. My skirt was around my waist before I could stop him, and then he lifted me up against the wall, pinning me there with his body.

His strength was effortless, and the hard flex of his muscles as he held me tapped into a very feminine part of me, making me shiver with delight. It was insane that

I should like this—his control, his dominance—but I couldn't help it. I *did* like it.

He shifted, pushing his lean hips insistently between my thighs, and because his jeans were open I could feel his cock, hard and hot, pressing against the soaking-wet fabric of my panties. The sensation was a lightning burst in my head…a shock of sensation overloading every nerve ending I had.

My mouth opened beneath his as I gasped, my hips rocking, pushing against him, and he muttered a vicious-sounding curse against my lips.

His fingers curled into the waistband of my panties, jerking hard, tearing through the lace. Then they were gone and his fingers were between my thighs, sliding through the slick folds of my pussy, finding my clit and circling in hard, tight circles.

I stiffened, unable to stop a desperate, choked sound escaping my throat. His touch was electric, the pleasure white-hot—unlike anything I'd ever felt before.

The sheer intensity of it hooked into the panic that was simmering below the surface, frightening me. My hands were on his chest, wanting to push him away, to stop this, but he eased one finger into me, then another, spread them apart, stretching me.

'Smoke… Oh, God…' I couldn't stop the words pouring out of my mouth. 'Jesus… Please… Smoke, I can't… I don't…'

His mouth was on mine again, kissing me hungrily, and his fingers were sliding deeper into my pussy. I shuddered, the hot wall of muscle beneath my palms searing me like the element on a stove. I was going to catch fire. I was going to burn alive right here in his arms.

His mouth moved to my jaw, down my throat, his teeth closed around the cords of my neck. 'You're so fucking wet.'

His voice was dark as midnight, husky and rough.

'So fucking tight. I knew you would be. I just knew it.'

He drew his hand back, sliding his fingers out, then back in, again and again, fucking me slowly, making me pant and gasp and writhe in his arms.

'You want my cock, kitten? Tell me you want it.' His voice got impossibly deeper. '*Beg* me for it.'

I couldn't breathe. It was like everything in me was drawn so tight the slightest breath would shatter me into a thousand pieces. Yet I wanted to move. I wanted to end this desperate ache, this need that was eating me alive.

I knew he was going to do it—fuck me right here in this hallway, where anyone could see us. And I didn't care. I just wanted this hunger to be gone.

'I w-want your cock,' I stuttered hoarsely. 'I want it right now.'

'Where do you want it?'

His fingers curled inside me, his thumb moving in a slow, slick circle over my clit.

I groaned. 'I want it in my pussy. Please, Smoke. *Please...*'

He shifted again, his fingers sliding out of me, making me tremble at the loss. While he held me against the wall he reached behind him to his wallet, deftly extracting a condom packet one-handed, before letting the wallet fall carelessly to the floor. He ripped the packet open with his teeth, discarding the wrapper and rolling the latex down. Then he gripped my thighs hard and positioned himself.

I could feel the head of his cock press against the entrance of my pussy, and I shook so hard it felt like I was going to come apart right there and then.

'Cat.'

My name was a harsh order.

'Fucking *look* at me.'

I did, but the expression on his face was so intense I could hardly stand it. Hunger and desperation and also anger. An anger I didn't understand.

His hips flexed and he was pushing into me, my slick flesh was parting before him, stretching around him, and the feel of him tipped me off the ledge I was only barely clinging to. The orgasm crashed over me, a massive shudder shaking my body as I cried out, lights bursting behind my eyes.

He didn't even pause, sliding deep inside me, holding me fast with my legs wrapped around his lean waist, the unbelievable heat of his body between my thighs.

I groaned at the sensation of him inside me, because he was big and it had been a long time since I'd had sex. Not to mention the fact that the aftershocks of my orgasm were like tiny bolts of electricity arcing from nerve ending to nerve ending, sensitising every part of me.

Then he was drawing his hips back, driving into me deep and fast and wild. Each thrust slammed me hard into the corner. I arched in his arms, shocked as that tight, impossible ache began to build again, the sharp need coiling tighter with each slide of his cock inside me. I gripped his T-shirt, my fingers fisting in the cotton, panting and then groaning again as he tilted my hips and changed the angle of his thrusts, so the base of his cock was grinding against my clit.

My head fell back against the wall, pleasure rising higher and higher, and the sounds of his ragged breathing and his sharp, hard grunts as he fucked me filled the space between us.

I'd never imagined it would be like this. Not with him. I'd never imaged this with him at all. And the worst part was knowing that it wasn't something we could pretend hadn't happened. We couldn't ignore it.

It was fierce, incendiary. It was going to change everything.

I said his name a thousand times, over and over, my voice so hoarse it didn't sound like mine. Then, when I didn't think I could bear it any more, he jerked my hand away from its death grip on his T-shirt and forced it down between my legs.

I tried to resist, for what reason I didn't know, but he was too strong, forcing my fingers to where we were joined, to feel my own wet pussy stretched around the thick, hard length of his cock. To feel the slick glide of him as he pulled out, the give of my flesh as he pushed back in.

'Feel me, kitten. This is *me*, inside *you*.' He held my fingers there, flexing his hips with each word to prove his point. 'This is me *fucking* you.'

I groaned, trembling so hard I thought I would break, the dirty words as much of a turn-on as the feel of his cock sliding into me.

My best friend. Fucking me in the hallway, where anyone could see us.

He moved his hand, urging my fingers higher, to my clit.

'Touch yourself,' he ordered harshly. 'I want you coming all over my cock in five seconds.'

I obeyed without thought, my fingers stroking my clit over and over as he fucked me hard against the wall until I was desperate and shaking and raw. And it didn't even take five seconds. In three I screamed his name into the silence of the hallway, my eyes shut tight as the sensation swept over me, annihilating me completely.

Dimly I felt him move harder and faster, his rhythm wild and out of control, and then he bent his head, turning his face into my neck. And he bit me hard as orgasm took him, too.

CHAPTER TWELVE

Smoke

I DIDN'T WANT to move. I wanted to stay there, my head turned in to her neck, inhaling the musky scent of aroused Cat and sex, with my dick buried so deep inside her I felt like I was part of her. She was panting, her body shaking, her legs wrapped tight around my waist, and I simply held her there, losing myself in the smell and feel of her.

I'd fantasised about her for years, and yet all those fantasies hadn't even come close to the reality. To the pressure of her mouth as she'd sucked me. To the tight, wet heat of her pussy around my cock. To the salty taste of her skin as I'd bitten her neck. So fucking good. So fucking intense.

I couldn't remember the last time I'd come so hard, and even now, two orgasms later, I was already getting hard for her again. But I didn't want to do anything more here in the clubhouse. I wanted to get her back to a bed, where I could take my time, undress her, taste every inch of her delicious body before sinking into her again. Fucking her slow, fucking her fast. Driving us both insane.

This was going to happen again, and soon, and I wasn't going to take no for answer. Not now that I'd felt how wet she'd been or heard her scream my name in my ear as she'd come.

Her hands pushed at my chest and, reluctantly, I slid out of her, letting her down onto the floor. She was shaky on her feet and had to keep her hands braced on my chest, which was fucking satisfying.

It was *all* so fucking satisfying.

For so many years she hadn't even noticed the fact that I was a man, and yet tonight, when she'd come to a stop in the hallway and turned to face me, I'd known that she'd noticed. That she'd run from what was happening around the bonfire was *because* she'd noticed. Which had made my decision real simple.

She'd gone down on her knees when I'd asked her to. Begged for my cock when I'd ordered her to. And then she'd come, screaming, exactly when I'd told her to.

She'd wanted it, whether she liked it or not. She'd wanted it. She'd wanted *me.*

Her head was bent, her dark hair hiding her face, but I didn't make her look at me—not yet. Instead I dealt with the condom in a nearby wastebasket and tucked myself back into my jeans. Then I pulled down her skirt, smoothing it over her thighs, covering her up.

She tried batting away my hands, but I ignored that bullshit. She was mine now, and if I wanted to take care of her I was going to take care of her—no goddamn arguments.

'Smoke…'

My name sounded all husky and raw.

'Can we just—'

'No,' I interrupted. 'Don't say another fucking word, Cat.'

Sliding a finger beneath her chin, I tipped her head up so she had to look at me. Her cheeks were deeply flushed, her green eyes dark, tendrils of black hair sticking to her forehead and neck. She looked shell-shocked, and I was asshole enough to get a kick out of it.

'I'm taking you back home. Now.'

Her mouth opened, but I put a finger on her soft lips, silencing her.

'What did I say about another fucking word?'

A muscle flexed in her jaw but she remained silent. Good girl.

I made sure our clothing was all good, then I took her hand and held it tight, turning and heading back down the corridor towards the club's exit.

Christ, I couldn't stop thinking about it. About her mouth and the feel of her body against mine. The little movements she'd made and her soft, desperate sounds of pleasure. I glanced down at her as we walked, watching the ebb and flow of colour in her cheeks, and I knew she was thinking the same thing.

But she didn't look back at me, which told me everything I needed to know about her feelings: she regretted it and it was obvious.

My chest tightened but I ignored it. If she thought we were going back to nothing but friendship, she was shit out of luck. She was *mine*. She was *my* property and I was going to have her every way I could.

Nothing about this was going to be pretend—not any more.

A couple of people asked where we were going, but I ignored them, too.

Outside, I put her on my bike and we left the club,
riding through the dark city streets. Her arms around
my waist were a special kind of torture, as was the
feel of her heat against my back, and by the time we
rolled up outside her apartment I was hard enough to
hammer nails.

But I'd decided I was going to give her space tonight.
Just one night to let what had happened between us sink
in. Because tomorrow I had plans. And they sure as shit
didn't include keeping my distance.

The babysitter—a friend of Red's old lady—was surprised to see us and no wonder. We were probably way
earlier than she was expecting. But I paid her for the
whole night, and apparently Annie had been good, so
everyone was happy.

Cat disappeared into Annie's room as I paid the
babysitter and didn't come out after the woman had
left. Probably didn't want to face me after what had
happened in the hallway and, hell, I couldn't blame
her. She hadn't been expecting it. Unluckily for her, I
didn't have any problem with dealing with the fallout.

Closing the door after the babysitter, I went down the
narrow hallway to Annie's bedroom and stood in the
doorway. Sure enough, Cat was sitting on Annie's bed,
stroking her hair. The nightlight threw shadows everywhere, its shade with cut-outs scattering stars onto the
ceiling, and the only sound was Annie's gentle, deep
breathing.

It was a peaceful picture. A beautiful one. It made
the tightness in my chest get even tighter—because this
was mine. This was my family. One I never thought I'd
ever have, never thought I'd even want.

After the shit had gone down with my father—after

he'd made my mother's life and mine a living hell—I'd decided I didn't want a wife. Didn't want kids. Didn't want a family. But it had been Cat who'd showed me that a family didn't have to be about fists and shouting. That it could be about respect, about love.

Until you took him out.

Yeah, there was that. My soul wasn't clean and I knew it. Yet somehow, clean soul or not, I had a family right here. A woman I would have moved heaven and earth for and a kid who wasn't mine and yet I'd lay down my life for her.

I wasn't going to give this up for anything. And if anyone tried to take Annie and Cat away from me, they'd have to prise them from my cold, dead hands.

Maybe she sensed me standing there, because Cat turned her head and her eyes met mine. I said nothing, just leaned against the doorframe, my hands in my pockets. Letting her know that I wasn't going anywhere in a hurry and that she couldn't escape me.

She flushed and turned away, leaning over to give Annie a kiss before rising to her feet. Giving her daughter one last look, she came towards me, and I could tell she was gathering her courage because her chin came up and her green eyes didn't flicker away from mine.

She said nothing as she went past me and didn't stop, heading out into the hall, so I followed on behind, watching the sway of her butt in that tight-fitting pencil skirt. Fuck, what had I been thinking about keeping my distance tonight? I wanted to bend her over the nearest hard surface, shove that goddamn skirt out of my way and bury myself so deep in her pussy she'd feel me for days.

But I knew Cat. I knew she was going to need at least

a night to get her head around this. A night for her body
to understand what it needed.

Me.

In the lounge she turned to face me, folding her arms,
all defensive, but I didn't stop. There weren't going to
be any damn lectures about how we needed to forget
all about this, put it behind us, make like it didn't happen. No—fuck that. She was my property now, and that
meant I got to call the shots.

'Smoke—' she began.

But I walked straight up to her, grabbing her hips
and pulling her in nice and tight, feeling the heat of her
perfect little pussy against my aching dick.

'No,' I said. 'Don't speak. Don't say a fucking word.'

Her jaw tensed and her mouth settled into a hard line.
But she didn't talk.

'Here's what's going to happen,' I went on, pressing my fingers against her hips, feeling her warmth
and softness, letting myself enjoy it. 'I'll leave you to
sleep alone tonight and I'll take the couch. But tomorrow you're taking the day off, and after Annie's gone
to school, you and me are going to have a little talk.'

She didn't try to pull away, but neither did she soften
against me. Her whole body was tense. She was holding herself rigid.

'And I guess when you say "little talk" you mean…?'

'Fucking, Cat.' No point in mincing words or pretending otherwise. 'You and I will be fucking.'

Her cheeks flamed. 'Well, I guess that's clear.' Her
voice was heavy with sarcasm. 'Nothing like reducing
it to the level of a porno.'

'I don't recall you having a problem with it when
I had you screaming in my ear in the damn hallway.'

She flushed even deeper, biting her lip and looking away.

I knew what was going on. She was doing what she always did when she was scared, which was to get snarky and defensive. Sadly, I wasn't going to be putting up with that bullshit.

'I'm not going to let you push me away.' I moved my thumbs back and forth over her hips, stroking her, keeping up that physical contact. 'Not any more. This is how it's going to be—starting tomorrow. You and me. Together.'

A lock of silky black hair fell over her face, hiding her expression as she looked down at her feet. 'I thought... I thought all this was supposed to be pretend.'

'It was *supposed* to be.' I didn't want to hide the truth from her—not now that we'd crossed the line. 'Then I changed my mind.'

'Why?' She still wouldn't look at me. 'Since when did things change?'

I looked down at the light glossing her black hair, at her lashes dark against her cheeks like splashes of black ink. Christ, I was turning into a fucking poet.

'They never changed. Not for me. I've always wanted you, kitten. *Always*.'

Her head came up sharply, her eyes wide, the look in them shocked as hell. 'What? But...' She blinked, the shock giving way to confusion. 'Really? You never said anything... I mean, I never got the impression that...' She stopped. 'Seriously, Smoke?'

But I was done for the night, and I suspected so was she. We could have all this out in the morning, when the shock had worn off.

'Tomorrow,' I said shortly. 'We'll talk about this to-morrow.'

A spark of green temper flared in her gaze. 'In be-tween all the fucking, you mean?'

She was *such* brat… Jesus Christ.

I lifted my hand, took her little chin in between my thumb and forefinger, holding her still. 'Maybe.' I kept my voice quiet. 'But only if you're a very good girl and do exactly as you're told.'

She snorted, like she was still my friend and we were kidding around with each other. But it was time she stopped thinking that shit, so I bent my head and kissed her hard, pushing my tongue into her hot mouth, silencing her.

A tremble shook her and she made a soft, desperate noise. Then she tipped her head back further, letting me kiss her deeper, her tongue meeting mine and slid-ing along it. It was a taste and a tease and a taunt all in one. Her hands were pressed against my chest, there was the scent of musk and Cat filling my senses, and suddenly I didn't want to wait till morning. I wanted her again—right the fuck *now*.

But she'd been leading me around by my dick for years and I was sick of it. It didn't matter that she hadn't known I wanted her. I didn't give a fuck how unfair or otherwise that was. *I* was the one in charge from now on and that was how it would stay.

I lifted my head, ignoring her soft moan of protest, and with my stupid fucking cock aching like it hadn't been inside her only an hour ago, I stepped back and away from her. 'Time for bed, kitten.'

An expression I couldn't read flashed over her face, then it was gone. She lifted a shoulder like she didn't give a shit—which made her a damn liar, considering her cheeks were flushed and her mouth looked full and swollen.

'I'll get you a pillow and a blanket,' she muttered, and turned away, heading out of the lounge.

A minute or two later she was back, a pillow in one hand, a blanket in the other, and going over to the couch, making a production of putting the pillow down and laying the blanket out flat.

Once she'd finished she made an awkward gesture towards the couch. 'There. It's done.'

A silence fell and I let it hang, because I was being a prick and enjoying the way the tension between us made her blush even more. Another sign that our friendship really was dead and gone.

Maybe I should have felt regret about that, but I didn't. Our friendship had been built on lies anyway— or at least for me it had been. The lie that I didn't want to make her mine in every way that counted.

Yeah, I was risking everything on this. But, then again, how much of a risk could it truly be? I wasn't going to let her go. Not now. Not ever.

Pushing my hands into my pockets, I met her gaze. 'Goodnight, Cat.'

She held it. 'Goodnight, Dane.'

Then she turned around and walked out.

CHAPTER THIRTEEN

Cat

I DIDN'T SLEEP all night. I was exhausted, yet my body was buzzing and my mind wouldn't stop replaying what had happened with Smoke over and over.

I shut my eyes, willing the images away, but they wouldn't go.

My body ached, my pussy was throbbing, my nipples were in hard, tight points. Pressing against the tank top I'd pulled on to sleep in.

'Fucking, Cat. You and I will be fucking.'

I turned my head into the pillow, trying and failing to find a cool spot, my skin feeling like it was on fire.

Crazy. I'd gone all these years without being attracted to Smoke, yet now I couldn't sleep because I couldn't stop thinking about tomorrow, about what we were going to do together.

It terrified me.

Shit, if the sex had been bad, we might have been able to put it behind us, carried on as normal. But the sex hadn't been bad. It had been…incredible. And there was no way we could put that behind us—no way in hell.

It was going to change things and they would never be the same again.

I squeezed my eyes shut tighter. No, I wasn't going to fucking cry about it. *I wasn't.*

'I've always wanted you, kitten.'

Oh, God, that look in his dark gaze. The one that went straight through me, that pinned me to the ground with a truth so sharp and so obvious I was amazed I hadn't seen it before.

Or maybe I simply hadn't wanted to look.

He'd wanted me all that time and it made me so shit-scared I could hardly breathe. He had to stay a friend—I *needed* him to stay a friend. Because anything more—like love—that was bullshit. It was *all* bullshit. Love was a lie, and in the end it always, *always* let you down.

Love had deserted my mom in the end, and in the end it had made her desert me.

And love always hurt—like Justin hurt me.

Relationships sucked and I didn't want one. But friendship—that was strong. That was true.

Friends never let you down—like Smoke had never let me down—and that was what I wanted. What I needed.

Except Smoke clearly had other ideas.

I was fucked. Literally.

I flung an arm across my hot face, trying to settle, but the memory of how I'd knelt before him and taken his dick into my mouth grabbed me, and this time I let myself fall into it, feeling the power of it…

Somewhere in the middle I must have fallen asleep, because the next thing I knew I felt something hot lying across my face. In fact I felt hot all over.

I opened my eyes to find the sun streaming through

a crack in the curtains and fully over my bed, in a way it never did when I woke at 6:00 a.m.

I groaned and turned to look at the clock.

Holy shit—it was *nine*. What about Annie? What about school? I'd never slept in like this before. Never.

Cursing, I hauled myself out of bed and flung open the door, stumbling down the hallway to Annie's bedroom only to find it empty. Oh, God, where was she?

I went back along the hall and into the lounge, trying not to feel frantic about the heavy silence that lay over the apartment. The living area was empty, too; the blanket Smoke had slept in was folded neatly on the end of the couch.

On the coffee table was a piece of paper with some writing on it.

I snatched it up.

Took Annie to school and you've called in sick.
Back soon. Be ready.

Jesus, the bastard really was handling all this, wasn't he?

A shiver snaked down my spine and it wasn't fear. In fact it felt horribly like anticipation.

Irritated, I scrunched the paper up into a ball. Because there was no way. It wasn't happening. I didn't want some guy swanning in and taking over my life the way Justin had. Telling me what to do and expecting me to be grateful. Even if he was my best friend.

What was going to happen was me sitting down with Smoke and telling him the truth. That I couldn't be more than friends with him. He knew my background…knew why my friendship with him was so important. He'd understand, surely? He *had* to.

Sighing, I dropped the balled-up paper and headed to the bathroom for a quick cold shower. Then I wandered back into the bedroom, wrapped in a towel, pulling open drawers and trying to decide what to wear.

It took me a moment to realise what I was doing.

I *never* stood in front of my drawers debating over clothes. I simply pulled on what was appropriate for work or what was comfortable for home. That was the extent of it.

Yet here I was, looking at the contents of my drawers with my head full of Smoke. Wondering what to wear that he'd like. Wondering what would make me look sexy.

Feeling like an idiot, I dropped the towel and reached for my usual jeans and T-shirt, pulling them on and resolutely not looking in the mirror.

Turning to the door to head out in search of coffee, I nearly had a heart attack when I found Smoke's black eyes staring back at me, the length of his hard, muscular body filling the doorframe.

I blushed the moment I met his gaze, a wave of heat rolling through me as every single one of last night's memories descended on me like a ton of bricks.

'F-fuck, you gave me a fright,' I stuttered. 'I didn't hear you come in.'

He lifted a shoulder. 'Yeah, sorry about that.'

Resisting the urge to tug at my hair or my T-shirt, I stuck my hands in my back pockets. 'Um…thanks for taking Annie to school. I guess I kind of slept in.'

He didn't move, staring at me with such intensity it

was like an X-ray, memorising me right down to my bones.

'No worries. You seemed like you needed it.'

An awkward silence fell, which he made no move to break—the asshole.

'I...I need to talk to you,' I said, not knowing how to begin and irritated that he wasn't giving me any help.

He didn't look surprised by this. 'Sure.' He turned. 'Come out to the living room.'

Pausing to grab a hair tie and put my damp hair in a ponytail, I followed him down the hallway, coming out to find him sitting in the middle of the couch with his arms along the back of it and his legs stretched out in front of him.

He was in his usual T-shirt and jeans, both black, his cut on over the top, and I could feel my heart literally slow and come to a dead stop because of the way he was sitting: his long, lean body all stretched out, so fucking arrogant. So fucking *hot*.

His T-shirt was pulled tight over his chest, highlighting the width and shape of the perfect musculature beneath. Tight over his shoulders, too, with the cotton moulding to the broad, powerful shape of them. He was strong enough he'd been able to lift me against the wall the night before like I weighed nothing...

My throat constricted, my breathing shallow.

I couldn't stop staring at his body, at the lean hips and muscular thighs. I remembered what he'd felt like against me, how hot his skin had been...

Asshole. It was like he'd turned something on inside me and now I couldn't turn it off.

He stared back, black eyes burning with the same

dark flame I'd seen in them in that hallway as I'd knelt at his feet.

'Strip,' he said flatly.

I blinked. 'W-what did you say?'

'Take off your clothes. *Now.*'

A helpless shiver broke over me. 'I thought we were going to talk.'

'We are. You can talk and I'll listen. But I want you naked.'

'But...but I—'

'That's how it's going to be from now on, kitten. We compromise. I get what I want and so do you.' His sensual mouth hardened. 'Now, take your fucking clothes off, or I'll take them off for you.'

Anger flared in my gut—reflexive, bonfire bright. Where the *hell* did he get off, ordering me around in my own home?

Yet there was another part of me—a part I'd only discovered the night before—that liked the freedom of doing nothing but obeying him. That was tired of having do everything all the time. Tired of having to shoulder the responsibility of bringing up a child on my own. That wanted someone else to make the decisions and take charge. Just for a little while.

It felt weak to give in to it. Like I was making myself vulnerable. And I knew what happened when I made myself vulnerable. Fists. Pain. My pride in tatters on the floor. I couldn't do it. Once had been enough last night.

But don't forget this is Smoke. He would never hurt you. And didn't you feel powerful last night?

I swallowed. It was still difficult for me to understand how that worked. How I could be on my knees and yet feel strong? But there was no doubting that was how I'd felt the night before. I could do it again, couldn't I?

Of course you can. You want to. Don't deny it.

Yeah, I did want to. A deep part of me wanted more of that—his hands and his mouth and his cock—no matter how wrong it was. No matter how scared it made me feel. The switch was firmly turned to On, and it looked like nothing was going to flip it back.

'Don't be a chickenshit, Cat.'

His low voice was a rumble I felt in my chest, taunting me the way he always used to when I baulked at doing something I was scared of.

He would never force me. He would never hurt me. He was a totally different man from Justin. A totally different man from my father.

Yet I was still scared.

I didn't want anything to change between us.

But then, of course it already had.

'What if I don't want this?' I asked. 'What if I want to talk without anything else?'

'Then I'm walking out of here,' he said without hesitation.

'Does that mean you'd walk out on Annie, too?'

Something even darker flickered in his eyes. 'Don't you fucking *dare* use Annie like that. You know I'd rather die than let anything happen to that kid.'

Shame crept over my skin, a creeping, prickling heat, and before I could stop myself the words just came out of me. 'I'm scared, Smoke.'

He didn't move, and the look on his face didn't soften. But the darkness in his eyes lessened slightly. 'I know you are. But I won't hurt you, kitten. You know I'd rather die than do that.'

I don't know what it was—maybe it was merely the reassuring sound of his voice, the normality of it. The voice of my friend. But the fear inside me ebbed…the tension eased.

And before I was even conscious of having made a decision my hands reached for the hem of my T-shirt and I was pulling it up and over my head and unclipping my bra and letting it fall. It had been a long time since I'd undressed in front of a guy, so I kept my attention on my hands as I undid the button on my jeans and slid down the zipper. Then I pushed down the denim, taking my panties with it.

It felt weird, undressing for my best friend. And when I stepped out of my jeans I found I still didn't want to look at him. My heartbeat was so fast, so loud, my skin felt raw and exposed. I wanted to cover myself, but kept my hands at my sides.

I wasn't a fucking coward. I wasn't.

Raising my head, I forced myself to look at him.

The expression on his face shook me all the way down to my soul.

It was so intense. So hungry. As if he'd never seen a naked woman in all his life.

A feeling swept through me—the same one I'd felt the night before. A feeling of power, of strength.

He wanted me. He was desperate for me.

I straightened, threw my shoulders back, and his gaze dropped to my breasts, then down further. A stain of red appeared on his high cheekbones.

'Come here,' he ordered, his voice thickened and rough.

I hated being told what to do, and yet I found myself going to him all the same. Like there was a collar around my neck and he held the leash, drawing me closer and closer.

I watched his face as I got nearer, watched him watch me, my heartbeat racing. My nipples had hardened and I could feel slickness between my legs, the heavy ache of desire making my breathing short and fast.

There was a part of me that didn't want him to see me so obviously turned on by him, but after last night that ship had sailed. I couldn't hide it. And he certainly didn't bother, making no effort to conceal the long, thick outline of his cock pressing against his zipper.

Breathless, I stopped in front of his outstretched legs, looking down at him. 'So?' I said awkwardly. 'Here I am.'

He didn't move and only patted his lap. 'Facing me, kitten.'

He definitely wasn't going to make this easy for me, was he? Facing him meant kneeling astride him and looking into his eyes…meant being vulnerable to him. And he knew it.

That challenge glittered in his black gaze—the one I couldn't refuse. So I moved towards him, climbing into his lap and spreading my thighs so I could straddle him. He made no move to help me, his attention dropping to my swaying breasts as I gingerly settled myself astride him.

My cheeks flamed. I wasn't used to this—to being naked in front of him while he was fully dressed, to him watching me so intently. Then I noticed that the lines of his gorgeous face were pulled taut and his mouth set hard. His body beneath mine was rock hard, as if every muscle was clenched tight.

He was holding himself back.

The realisation made my embarrassment fade, leaving me aware of how rough the denim of his jeans felt against the insides of my thighs, of how hot he was, like lying right next to a roaring fire.

He didn't take his eyes off me, staring unspeaking as he lifted his hands and settled them lightly on my hips. I trembled, his touch setting off electric shocks that spider webbed all over my skin, catching me in a fine net of heat I couldn't escape from.

I tried to take a breath, but it sounded more like a gasp, and I realised with a start, as his fingers tightened on my bare flesh, that he was pushing me down onto him with slow, irresistible pressure.

Unable to do anything else, I let him push until I was sitting properly on him. Until the soft, vulnerable flesh of my pussy was pressed against the denim of his jeans and the rigid outline of his cock underneath it. Just that bit of friction caused the net of heat to tighten, pulling against my skin, making me tremble even harder.

'You wanted to talk?' His voice was soft and rough. 'Then let's talk.'

Strange to sit naked on him like this and look into his inky eyes. I couldn't get rid of the almost overwhelming urge to move on him. To rub myself against the hard outline of his dick. Pull up his T-shirt, touch his smooth, hot skin. I wanted to kiss him, drive him crazy, make him feel the same terrifying desperation he made me feel.

But I didn't. My voice had got stuck in my throat and I couldn't speak. Dumb. I'd never been a woman who let herself get overwhelmed by a man—not even when I'd been in love with Justin—and yet apparently all I needed was to be sitting naked in Smoke's lap and I couldn't say a word.

'You don't trust me, do you?'

I could hear the accusation in his voice, could hear the hurt, too. It made me hurt in response. Jesus, all I seemed to be able to do lately was hurt him.

'No,' I said thickly. 'It's not that.'

'Yeah, it is.'

His thumbs moved on my hips, stroking me, sending flames over my skin.

'If you trusted me this wouldn't be scary.'

I met his searing black eyes. The intense heat in them nearly stole my breath. 'I do trust you. It's just...' I stopped, trying to get my thoughts together. 'It's scary because you're my closest friend. You're all I have. And I don't want to fuck that up. I don't...'

My voice shook, but I knew I was going to have to say it. I had to make myself.

'I don't want to lose you.'

His jaw was tight, his mouth hard, and the look he gave me was unrelenting.

'Yeah, and that's what I mean by not trusting me. Do you seriously think I would ever leave you? I've been your friend for over twenty fucking years, Cat. Nothing's ever going to make me go.'

It felt like he'd taken my heart in those big, warm, strong hands of his and was slowly squeezing it.

'Sex changes things. Sex makes things—'

'Don't confuse this with what happened between your parents, or between you and that asshole Justin. This is different and you know it. Fuck, *I'm* different.'

Of course he was different. Rationally, I knew that. But emotionally I was so fucked up I couldn't shake the sense that I was getting in too deep, that if I let him he'd overwhelm me. That I'd somehow end up being powerless and alone.

'I know, but…' I struggled to articulate it. 'This chemistry between us… It's kind of insane. And it scares me. I hate feeling out of control, and last night… what we did…' I stopped, not wanting to say anything more.

Something intent and angry glittered in his eyes. 'Have I ever once given you a reason not to trust me?'

'I…'

'*Have* I, Cat?'

My throat tightened, because no, he hadn't. 'It's not you, Smoke. It's me.'

His mouth hardened. 'Say it.'

'No,' I croaked. 'You've never given me a reason not to trust you.'

'No, I fucking haven't.'

Unexpectedly, he shifted beneath me, giving a subtle roll of his hips that made the denim of his jeans rub against my pussy and the hard outline of his dick push against my clit, making me shudder helplessly.

'This chemistry *is* insane and I want it. What we did last night—I want that, too. Every goddamn night. And you know what else? If you trusted me, you wouldn't worry about being a little out of control.'

The net of heat pulled even tighter over my skin, trapping me. 'S-Smoke…'

'Over twenty years and you still don't trust me.'

His hold on my hips firmed and he exerted pressure, holding me down on his lap.

'That means I'm going to have to teach you a lesson.'

He rolled his hips again, grinding slowly, making me

ride the hard ridge of his dick, pressing it against my
clit. I groaned as the unbearable pleasure began to ripple outwards and my face got hot. Everything got hot.

'I want you out of control, kitten,' he murmured, his
breath feathering against my ear. 'I want you screaming. I want you to lose it so that you understand I'll always be there to hold you when you fall.'

His hips moved again, sending another electric jolt
through me.

'I'll always be there to keep you safe.'

I gasped, desperate to pull away from the overwhelming sensation, but he held me down and all I
could do was sit there as his hips rolled again, rubbing
the rough denim against my achingly sensitive flesh,
the ridge of his cock hitting my clit. Over and over.

Shaking, I lifted my palms and pressed them flat to
his chest, tipping my head against his shoulder. But one
of his hands tangled in my hair, pulling my head back
instead, and his mouth covered mine in a hot, wet, open-
mouthed kiss. The other slid over my hip to stroke the
curve of my butt, his fingers trailing around and down
to the inside of my thigh, his fingertips lightly brushing the slick folds of my pussy.

I groaned, feeling his fingers teasing as he ground
against my aching clit, as he kissed me, slick and hot,
nipping and biting, exploring my mouth with a single-
minded mastery I had no hope of resisting.

Then those teasing fingers moved higher, to the
crease of my ass, slipping between. I froze, every muscle clenching hard with shock, as he pressed one fingertip against the tight ring of muscle. But he didn't
stop, pushing and pushing, his finger sliding relentlessly inside me.

I shuddered, gasping into his mouth as an intense, dirty kind of heat swept over me, making me sweat. He kept moving his hips, rubbing his dick against my swollen, wet flesh, and the pleasure become sharp, like the point of a knife. His finger pressed deeper... The roll of his hips was faster. He bit my lower lip—enough that the hurt was a bright spot of pain—and that made the pleasure even sharper.

My thighs were trembling and I had to close my eyes, pushing against his chest, trying to pull away from the finger in my ass, only to press my clit harder against the rigid line of his cock. Stars burst behind my lids—pinpricks of light in the darkness.

He tasted like coffee and smelled like sex, and a thick velvet blackness was wrapping itself around me. Making me move against him, with him, chasing the friction, chasing the climax I knew was just out of reach.

'You want to come. Don't you?' he whispered against my mouth, and the finger in my ass was moving slowly, lazily, as he ground his hard cock against my clit until I sobbed. 'You want to come so bad.'

My body was shaking like I had a fever, unbelievable pleasure roaring in my head. The hard points of my nipples were grazing his chest and that was almost too much to bear. I felt like I was drowning in sensation and helpless to stop it.

'Yes, please... Smoke...' My voice was so hoarse. 'I want it... I need it...'

'What do you want?' His finger pushed deeper, tearing a groan from my throat. 'Say it.'

'I want to...c-come.'

His hips moved in a slow circle and my fingers curled

into the fabric of his T-shirt as pleasure began to tear me apart.

'Do you trust me?'

'Yes… Oh, God…' Another agonising roll, even slower this time, the friction relentless, insane. 'I…t-trust you.'

His finger pulled out, then pushed back in, making me want to scream. 'Prove it to me.' His voice was rough, guttural. 'Give me control, kitten.'

The last shreds of a resistance I hadn't known was still there were torn away.

'Yes!' My voice was ragged and cracked. 'Take it. It's yours.'

He didn't wait. His hips pushed up at the same time as he pressed me down, and everything was squeezing me into a small, tight, hard ball. The pressure of his dick against my clit, the push of his finger in my ass, his hand on my hip, squeezing me so hard. And then, like a fist uncurling, it was released, the orgasm detonating inside me, making me push my head against his chest and scream.

Breaking me into pieces and leaving me shattered in his lap.

CHAPTER FOURTEEN

Smoke

I WAS SO hard I was in agony, but I didn't fucking care. The pain was worth it for the pleasure of holding a naked Cat in my arms as she came, screaming against my chest. I didn't let go, holding her as she shuddered, riding out the climax.

As her tremors faded I stroked her back, loving the feel of her satiny damp skin under my palm. She'd gone heavy and still, resting her forehead on my chest, her breathing ragged and loud in the silence of the room.

I bent to nuzzle her hair, the sweet smell of her shampoo almost drowned by the salt and musk of feminine arousal. I nearly growled, wanting that scent all over me—on my skin, in my mouth, every-fucking-where. I wanted to eat her alive, taste every inch of her, explore every part of her with my tongue and my fingers and my cock.

For too many years that had been an empty, hollow dream.

Not any more.

Now she was mine.

Now I could indulge every fantasy I'd ever had and

that reality—after years and goddamn years of trying
to resist—was almost overwhelming.

But we had the whole day. There was no rush, no
hurry. Even so, I was a greedy bastard, and there was
no way I was going to waste time doing nothing when
I could be doing something.

And right now that 'something' was getting inside
of Cat.

I eased her off my lap, handling her with care. 'I'll
be two seconds,' I murmured. 'Stay right here. Don't
fucking move.'

I didn't wait for a reply, getting up and going down
the hallway and into her small bathroom.

I soaked a washcloth in hot water, then went back
to the living room. She'd curled herself up at one end
of the couch, her face turned away, her cheek pressing
against her arm. She was hugging herself as if she was
cold, and that made my chest get tight.

I knew I'd been hard on her—knew that I'd pushed
her. Maybe I'd pushed too hard.

*Yeah, but that's what you do, isn't it? You always
push too fucking hard.*

Ignoring the voice in my head, I moved over to the
couch, sitting down and then pulling Cat back into my
lap. There was only a moment's tension before she relaxed, resting her cheek against my chest.

Gently, I coaxed her legs apart, checking the vulnerable flesh between them. As I'd thought, her little pussy
had been rubbed raw against the denim of my jeans,
and her skin was an angry red.

Fuck. I shouldn't have held her down so hard. Pissed
with myself, I stroked the washcloth lightly between her
thighs, hoping the heat would help. Her head fell back

against my arm, and there was a flash of green as she looked up at me from beneath her silky black lashes.

I met her gaze, the tightness in my chest easing. Something glowed in the depths of her eyes and it wasn't devastation, or fear, or any of the other things I realised I'd been half expecting. It was something warmer, fiercer.

'You bastard...' she murmured. 'I think you've broken me.'

But she wasn't broken—I could see that. I'd pushed her—and pushed her hard—but she was strong. Christ, she was probably stronger than I was when it came down to it. Women always were. Certainly my mother had been.

'Liar.' I moved the washcloth gently, watching her shiver in response. 'Broken is the last thing you are.'

Her mouth was swollen from the kisses I'd given her, and now it curved in a smile. I bent, brushing my lips over hers, the tip of my tongue dipping in to taste her purely because I could. Because I wanted to.

She didn't resist, opening her mouth beneath mine as if she'd been waiting for the moment.

So good. Fuck, she went straight to my head—sweet and hot like the best bourbon money could buy.

I could control myself. I wasn't a teenage boy. Yet one kiss from Cat and I almost came in my jeans.

Carefully I pushed her out of my lap, dropping the cloth, my hands shaking as I got to my feet and started ripping off my clothes. So much for not being in a rush.

On the coffee table was a plastic bag with the box of condoms I'd got from the drugstore and I reached for it, unable to get the damn thing open fast enough.

Cat watched me from the couch, her eyes wide,

staring as I ripped open a packet and got out the condom, rolling the latex down over my painfully hard
dick. Her eyes widened even further as I came over to
the couch, her gaze roaming over me like she'd never
seen me before in all her life.

There was heat in the green depths of her eyes and
it made me feel like a fucking god. Women liked me,
but Cat's appreciative stare was like gas down a fuel
line, sending my heartbeat into overdrive.

I turned her over onto her back and spread her legs
wide before kneeling between them. She gave a shiver
as I ran my fingers over her inner thighs, stroking her,
green lightning in her gaze.

'You okay?' I let my fingers trail further, through
the silky black curls of her pussy, brushing her soft,
wet flesh. 'Sore?'

The breath hissed in her throat, and a red flush
stained her cheekbones. 'A little.'

I was too far gone to stop, so I said, 'Let me know
if it's too much.'

I reached down, spreading her with my fingers and
easing the head of my cock into position. Then I leaned
over her, putting one hand beside her head, looking
down into her flushed face.

'Watch me, kitten. Don't take your eyes off me.'

I pushed into her, long and deep and slow, and the
hot, wet grip of her slit closed around me, holding me
so tightly I could hardly breathe.

So good. So goddamn good.

She moaned, her lashes fluttering, her back arching.
The sight was fucking erotic. Cat, naked, beneath me
at last…at last. Her nipples were tight and hard. Sweat
gleamed in the hollow of her throat. I looked further

down to where my cock had disappeared inside her, saw the wet pink flesh of her pussy spread apart.

'Fuck, *yes*.' I pushed her knees up and out, opening her wider so I could watch myself sink even deeper. 'Take me, kitten. Take it all.'

She groaned again and I slid one hand beneath her hips, lifting her, tilting her so I could get as deep inside her as I could.

'S-Smoke… I can't… I don't think…'

'Yes, you can.' I drew my hips back, watching the wet gleam of her pussy around my aching dick. 'You fucking can.'

Then I thrust in slowly, making us both groan as pleasure rippled outwards.

The urgency had faded now I was inside her and I wanted to take my time. Savour it. Savour *her*. Give her all the pleasure she deserved…make her scream my name over and over again.

Her fingers closed around my biceps, digging in the more deeply I settled inside her, and her head went back, exposing the arch of her throat. Sweat glittered on her skin, and her breathing shuddered in the space between us.

She was so fucking beautiful.

'This is the way it should have been, Cat.' My voice got hoarse as I drew my hips back in a long, lazy glide. 'And this is the way it's going to be from now on.'

I thrust in with the same lazy movement.

A ragged gasp escaped her. I felt her nails against my skin. 'I'm not sure… I can…handle this…'

I thrust again, taking my time, enjoying the sound of her ragged breath and the sight of the agonised pleasure on her face.

'You can handle anything, kitten.' Another deep thrust, teasing us both as her flesh gripped mine. 'You're so fucking strong.'

'I don't know...' She began to pant, her hips lifting. 'You might be...too much for me... Oh, God...'

Too much? No fucking way. This woman had had a child on her own. Had faced down that prick of an abusive ex. Had created a life for herself out of nothing. She could handle me—oh, yes, she damn well could.

It made me want to prove to her exactly how much she could take.

I paused and slid a hand beneath one of her knees, lifting it up and over my shoulder while keeping the other held wide, making her even more open to me. Then I leaned forward, pushing as deep as I could get.

'Oh...*fuck*...'

Cat's eyes squeezed shut. Her hands clenched on my shoulders, her nails scratching again, but that was all good. I wanted her marks on me. I wanted the scratches, the signs of the pleasure I'd given her. The pleasure that *only* I had given her.

I moved faster, pushing her against the arm of the couch with each thrust into that slick, perfect little pussy of hers.

'See what you can take? You can take everything I throw at you.'

It was starting to get to me now. The intensity of the sensation. The heat of her bare skin all silky and smooth against mine. The musky, salty scent of sex and Cat. Pleasure was uncoiling up my spine, roaring in my head like the sound of my Harley's pipes, and I wanted to go faster, to drive so deep and hard I lost myself.

She was mine. She was *all* mine.

'S-Smoke…' She twisted beneath me, her hips moving faster, rubbing herself against me. 'Oh… Jesus… Please…'

I upped the pace, loving the feel of her pussy clamping around my cock as I drove inside her, feeling the pressure of her leg over my shoulder and the slight pain of her nails in my back.

Her face was deeply flushed, her bottom lip between her teeth, and her eyes were tightly shut—black lashes against red cheeks, tears caught there, glittering like tiny diamonds. She was perfect…fucking perfect.

Except I wanted her to look at me.

I paused and reached down, gripping her chin in my hand. 'Eyes on me.'

Her lashes lifted. The green of her irises was now lost to the black of her pupils and it made me want to growl in satisfaction, because there was nothing but pleasure deep in that beautiful gaze of hers. No fear— not this time. And no looking away.

'You're mine.' My voice was guttural, unrecognisable, and I couldn't stop myself from repeating it. So we both knew exactly what was going on here. 'You're fucking *mine*.'

Then I bent and covered her beautiful mouth, pushing my tongue inside as I pushed my dick deep into her hot little pussy.

She shuddered, a moan vibrating in her chest. Then she began to kiss me back as hard as I was kissing her, her tongue sliding against mine, her body twisting, thrusting up to take me even as I was taking her.

I didn't want it to be slow any more. I wanted her harder, faster. Wanted the sound of her cries and the smack of my flesh against hers.

I wanted to fuck her into the middle of next week.

It became something like a fight—me trying to hold her down so I could fuck her hard while she thrust her hips up, trying to rub her clit against the base of my cock, kissing me hungrily, frantically.

Her nails scratched down my back and I swear she drew blood.

She drove me fucking crazy.

It got hotter, more desperate. I cupped the back of her head to protect her as I slammed her against the arm of the couch, her tits bouncing with each thrust, her cries loud in my ear. Then I turned my mouth into her neck, biting down on the delicate tendons at the side as she clenched hard around my cock.

Her skin tasted salty and sweet. I swear I thought I'd died and gone to heaven.

Another deep thrust. And another. And another.

Pleasure was like a fucking nightclub at the back of my head—a drumbeat that wouldn't let up. I tried to hold on, take it slow, make it controlled, but she was becoming frantic, clawing at me, sobbing and desperate.

I'd never experienced anything hotter in all my goddamn miserable life.

Yeah, cause you don't deserve it.

But no, I wasn't having any of that bullshit. Of course I deserved it. After all the bad shit I'd done in my life having Cat finally beneath me was something I'd never looked for, but now the moment was here I'd be damned if I let it slip through my fingers.

So I kept on moving, kept driving us both to the edge of insanity. And then, when she was sobbing my name, tears streaking her cheeks, our bodies slippery with sweat, I slid my hand between us, down to her small, swollen clit. I brushed my fingers over it. Once. Twice. Then I thrust hard, burying myself as deeply inside her as I could get.

Cat screamed my name, her pussy clamping down hard on my cock, her nails digging into my skin and her back arching like she'd been given an electric shock. Then she began to sob, her whole body shuddering as orgasm took over.

I held her tight, turning her face into my neck as I gave a couple more hard thrusts, my orgasm shooting up my spine and exploding out through the top of my head—the purest fucking pleasure I'd ever known.

And afterwards such complete... Jesus, I didn't have a word for it. Maybe it was peace. The kind of peace I'd felt in the moments after Dad took his last breath, when a weight had just lifted right off me. A weight I hadn't realised was there.

Fucked up to think *that* right now, but that's what I was. Fucked up.

I bent my head and buried my face in Cat's hair, inhaling the sweet scent of shampoo, of salt and musk and sex. Of home.

I was never going to let her go.

Never. Ever. *Ever.*

CHAPTER FIFTEEN

Cat

IT WAS THE second time that morning I'd come apart in Smoke's arms. The second time I'd screamed his name. The second time I'd been annihilated by pleasure.

The first time I'd been scared of what was happening between us.

Now I didn't give a fuck.

It was like he'd taken all the fear, all the doubt, all the uncertainty away, leaving me with just sensation. But then that was what Smoke did, wasn't it? He made everything okay—he always had.

It seemed ridiculous to me, now that I was lying wrapped tight in his arms, his face pressed into my hair, that I'd been so scared before—that I'd had so much difficulty trusting him. Because I should have. Of course I should have. I mean, I trusted him with my child. What was my heart in comparison?

Your heart?

Figure of speech. I loved Smoke. He was my best friend in the world, the person I counted on most. Of course I loved him. But I'd never been 'in love' with him. That had been a step I'd never wanted to take, a place I'd never wanted to go—not with him. Love was shit and I didn't want to stain our friendship with it.

Things are going to change now, though, aren't they? You've kind of taken a step in that direction.

Yeah, there was no denying it. Things *had* changed— and it wasn't even just the sex. He wanted us to be together the way an old lady was together with her old man—virtually married—and if I wanted Annie to stay safe, I wasn't going to get a choice about it.

So? He's a man who'll never hurt you, who'll do anything for you, who'll protect you and Annie, and give you astounding orgasms. What more could you want?

Good point. Something in me wanted that more than anything I'd ever wanted anything in my entire life, and yet something else kept resisting. I didn't know what it was—my daddy issues, my ex issues, or something else again—but I could feel it holding me back.

I didn't want to get hurt again—that was the main thing—and if I gave Smoke everything, the power he'd have over me...

His big, lean body shifted, the feel of his bare skin moving over mine, making my mouth go dry and scattering every thought in my head. He lifted his head, those dark eyes staring down at me. He was pressed against every inch of me, his still-semihard cock resting against the inside of my thigh. The heat of him was incredible, and the musky scent of aroused male filled the space around us.

I wanted to arch against him, rub myself all over him, trace his ink, run my hands over those powerful shoulders, feel all the hard-cut muscle of his pecs and then down to the corrugated lines of his abs. Explore every inch of his smooth, hot skin.

I'd never felt that way about a man. *Ever.* Not even
with Justin. Perhaps that should be a warning, and
maybe a day or two ago I would have listened to it.
But now…now I ignored it, looked up into his black
eyes and lost myself.

'You,' he said, his voice all rough and sexy, 'are fucking incredible.'

You're fucking mine.

The possessive note in those words should have had
me running for the hills—especially after Justin—but
when Smoke said them it was different. It made me
feel wanted, desired. It made me feel cared for. As if
for the first time I wasn't merely my father's unwanted
daughter or my mother's little mistake. I wasn't Justin's
punching bag. I wasn't even Annie's mom.

I was Smoke's old lady. I was Cat.

I touched his face, sliding a finger down his straight
nose and across one high cheekbone. Trailing it down
to his jaw and along the rough stubble of his morning beard, prickling against my fingertip, I reached his
mouth, traced his lower lip. It felt firm and yet soft—
the only soft thing there was about him.

'So are you.'

It didn't encompass what I felt, but it was true all the
same. He was. Absolutely fucking incredible.

He smiled, his mouth curving under my fingertip,
and the sight of it made my heart stretch out inside
my chest and shivers chase all over me. Hungry, sexy,
dangerous.

My best friend. My lover.

Gently, he took my fingertip between his strong
white teeth, nipping me, sending an intense jolt of sensation straight to my core.

'It's not over yet. We have the entire fucking morning. And I intend to use all of it.'

Even now, even like this, when there was nothing between us but skin, I blushed. 'Don't you have other stuff to do?'

'Nope. Like I said, I'm planning on doing nothing but fucking you.'

I blushed even harder—which was ridiculous. I'd heard him say worse stuff. Then again, it was never usually me he was talking about when he referred to fucking.

'Well, we've done that now, so—'

'What?' he demanded, his brows rising almost up to his hairline. 'We've "done that"? I don't fucking think so. I've got a lot of fantasies where you're concerned, Cat, and they don't include one vanilla missionary on the couch.'

I swallowed, feeling self-conscious and out of my depth. My sex life so far had been nothing to write home about, but it had been okay. I'd never had a lover like Smoke before—a man who took what he wanted. Who was raw, uninhibited and completely unselfconscious about anything. I was not any of that.

One corner of his mouth turned up, as if he'd read my mind. 'What? Still scared?'

'No, of course not,' I replied hotly, and he laughed at my rise to his obvious bait. I hit him lightly on one muscular shoulder. 'Don't be such an asshole. This is new for me. I need a bit of time to come to terms with it. I mean, you only just told me you've apparently wanted me for years.'

The wicked look on his beautiful face made my heart turn over in my chest.

'You don't need time,' he said.

And before I could say another word, he'd flipped me over onto my front, with him hot and hard and heavy pressed to my back.

'All you need is more of my fucking cock.'

I took a startled breath as his hand came down on the back of my neck, gently but firmly urging my head down onto the couch cushions, turning my face towards the door.

'You always have an answer, don't you?' My voice was starting to get husky… My heartbeat was speeding up.

'That's because I'm always right.'

He kept his hand there as his arm slid under me, pulling me up onto my knees, my butt in the air.

'I mean it, Smoke. I need time and—'

I broke off as he pushed his knees between mine, making me widen my stance, and the heavy heat of that cock pushing between my thighs and sliding along the slick flesh of my pussy made my legs tremble.

'Is this too much for you, kitten?'

He flexed his hips, his dick stroking the tender skin between my legs, its rounded head hitting my clit and drawing a groan from me. At the same time he kept that hand on the back of my neck, in a not so subtle domination.

'Tell me and I'll stop.'

Relentless pleasure was beginning to build again with every push of his hips, with every slide of his cock through the wet folds of my pussy.

But it wasn't pleasure I was afraid of. It was the loss of my control…the way I could feel my heart slipping

JACKIE ASHENDEN   163

from my fingers and falling straight into his waiting
palms.

It had always been there, this possibility. Just waiting for me to notice. I deliberately hadn't noticed. I'd
looked away.

I didn't want to fall for him—and not because of the
club. That was a smokescreen and I knew it—we both
did. I didn't want to fall for him because of what I could
lose. And it wasn't about the loss of our friendship.

It was about the loss of him.

I couldn't lose Smoke. I just couldn't.

Because you're in love with him already.

I shut my eyes tight. I couldn't think of that. I didn't
want to think of that. Better to concentrate on physical sensations. The slick, slow drag of his dick through
my folds. The scent of sex and sweat, of his need and
mine. The fabric of the sofa cushion beneath my cheek.

Yeah, so much better to think about that.

'Well?'

The word was rough, hard edged. He pulled back and
I felt the head of his cock press against my ass.

'What about this? Is this too much?'

I shuddered, my breathing catching.

He pressed a little harder, his free hand sliding
around and across my stomach, down between my
thighs, finding my clit and stroking me.

Pleasure stretched out, lazy and hot, and I panted,
watching the darkness behind my lids fissuring, crack-
ing.

'Cat?' A flick of his fingers against my aching clit.
'Answer me.'

I heaved in a breath. 'I…I…don't know…'

Another push and my flesh was parting, momentarily painful, making me shiver and groan, my muscles tightening in response. I didn't think I would ever want that, but it seemed like there were a lot of things I'd thought I wouldn't want, only to find I needed them more than my next breath.

Perhaps he knew, because a deep, husky laugh broke from him—the utter bastard. 'Thought as much. Don't worry. There'll be plenty of time for that later. Right now I haven't got much patience when it comes to getting inside you.'

He pulled away again, and this time a hint of anger and not a little bit of shame coiled through my relief. Jesus, backing away from this because I was scared meant I was being the goddamn chickenshit he'd accused me of being earlier.

And I wasn't. I *so* wasn't.

'I'm *not* scared.'

I wanted to prove it to him, backing up against him, pushing insistently, or at least as much as I could with his hand on my neck.

That hand firmed, stilling me. 'Stop,' he ordered quietly, and I did, unable to resist the gentle command in his voice. The pressure eased. 'You don't have to prove anything to me, Cat.'

'Don't I? Didn't you call me chickenshit before?'

He muttered something under his breath that sounded like a curse. 'I shouldn't have. I was a tool.'

His free hand moved to my back, stroking down my spine in soothing motion.

'I'm not fucking you in the ass right now anyway. I've got some lube, but you'll need preparation—and, like I said, I haven't got the patience right now. I'm not into pain—least of all yours.'

A blush worked its way up my throat to my cheeks. Not knowing what else to say and feeling ridiculous, I tried to sit up. But his hand was heavy on my neck again, keeping me where I was.

'Doesn't mean I'm not going to fuck you, though,' he murmured. 'So stay exactly like that. Don't move.'

The hand on my neck and the heat at my back disappeared as he got off the couch. I could have got up, too, if I'd wanted to. But he'd told me to stay there so I did, with my head on the couch cushions and my butt in the air, watching him as he went to get another condom from the box. All lithe, easy grace and fluid muscle, the Knights tattoo spread out on his back flexing as he tore open the packet and rolled the latex down.

The pulse of desire was back between my legs… hungry and empty.

Smoke turned and came back, kneeling behind me again, leaning over me, his hands coming down on either side of my head. The heat of his body was there once more, pressing against me… God, I loved the feel of him.

I shivered as I felt him shift, his right hand lifting from beside my head to touch my shoulder and then sliding down the curve of my spine. A long, gentle stroke to the small of my back and then up again. I arched into his hand like the kitten he called me, a ripple of pleasure making me lift my hips, press my butt insistently against him, wanting him.

He didn't seem to take the hint, just stroking me easy and slow. Then I felt the warmth of his breath on the small of my back.

I tensed. What the hell was he doing *now*?

His hands curved over my butt in a gentle caress,

moving lower between my thighs, easing my legs wide apart. And then, shockingly, his tongue pushed into me from behind—a hard, deep thrust.

I gasped, my fingers sinking deep into the couch cushions as a bolt of the most intense pleasure shot up my spine, exploding in my head. Instinctively I tried to move, but his hands gripped the backs of my thighs, holding me in place as he gave me another long lick, his tongue sliding inside me.

I groaned and shut my eyes as he did it again and again, tearing gasps from my throat, making my legs shake, making me want to lift my hips to give him better access. But he held me so tight I couldn't move. All I could do was stay on my hands and knees, sobbing with pleasure while he ate me from behind, begging him to end it.

But he didn't. Only when I was incoherent with pleasure did he stop, leaving me wet and throbbing and empty.

Straightening up to cover me again, he pushed his weight against my back, the heat of his groin against my butt.

Then he thrust his cock deep inside me. *Hard.*

I came instantly, screaming into the cushions, my pussy clenching hard around him as he slid in and out, slow and easy and deep. And he kept going as if he had all the time in the world, his fingers slipping around and underneath me to find my swollen, aching clit. Toying with me until I was shaking and gasping all over again.

I don't know how many times I came before he moved harder, faster, taking for himself what he'd given me. But there was one thing I was certain of.

He'd wrecked me.
He'd ruined me.
And I would never be the same again.

CHAPTER SIXTEEN

Smoke

As soon as I finished up the meeting I'd had with Keep—some shit to do with problems with The Demon's Share—I walked straight out of the clubhouse and headed for my Harley, impatience gnawing a hole in my gut.

It was near 5:00 p.m., and if that meeting meant I couldn't get to the jeweller before the store closed I was going to be pissed.

I had something important to pick up. Something I wanted to give to Cat.

It had been nearly two weeks since we'd got together, and living with her had only cemented the certainty deep inside me.

She was mine—every part of her. Her long glossy dark hair and her big green eyes. Her hot little pussy and her delicious tits. The way she kissed me when she came home from her day job and the way she snuggled up to me on the sofa as we watched TV. The way she unconsciously touched me and let her hand linger, trailing over my chest or my abs or my shoulders, as if she couldn't keep her hands off me.

She'd told me that morning after the club party that I'd ruined her. Well, she'd ruined me back.

Before, I buried my craving for her in other women, because I knew she'd never want me the way I wanted her. And I'd been okay with that. I'd handled it the only way I could.

But now I *had* her. Now I knew how she tasted when I kissed her mouth, when I pushed my tongue into her pussy. Now I knew how it felt to be balls-deep inside her, to have her legs wound around my waist and screaming my name in my ear.

Now I knew how good it was to have her curl up in my arms and put her head on my chest and fall asleep, as if she was safe, as if she trusted me completely...

Yeah, she'd ruined me.

There would be no one else for me.

That morning we'd had an argument about me handling her bills, paying her rent for the month, and then I'd made the mistake of mentioning that maybe we should find a new place to live. She'd been pissy, reminding me that this arrangement wasn't supposed to be permanent and that she wasn't going anywhere until the threat to Annie from Justin had been sorted out.

Except the 'arrangement' *was* permanent for me. This was real and it always had been.

I wanted to tell her there and then what I was planning—I'd been waiting because I wanted to give her some time to get used to having me around—but she'd cut me off because she had to go to work, telling me we'd talk about it tonight.

She was still scared. I could see it in her eyes. She was still doubting me—doubting us. So I decided to pay extra to get the ring I'd had made for her finished

that day. It would be proof of my commitment to her—
my promise that I'd never leave her. That she was stuck
with me for good.

What if she doesn't want to be stuck with you?

I revved the Harley, the thought making me growl
like the bike.

Too bad. She was mine, and I wasn't letting her go.

Picking up the ring from the jeweller didn't take long,
and then I was on my way back to Cat's apartment. She
was already home. I could hear her in the kitchen on the
phone as I walked in, talking to the sitter who looked
after Annie after school on the days I wasn't able to.

My pulse started doing crazy shit. The ring was
burning a hole in the pocket of my jeans, what-ifs were
spinning in my head, and I found myself pacing around
the room trying to calm myself the fuck down.

The territorial biker in me was never going to let her
go, regardless of what she wanted, but there was another
part of me—the friend—that wanted her to want that,
too. That wanted her to put on my ring and tell me that
she'd stay with me forever.

'Hey.'

I looked up at the sound of her voice to find her
standing in the doorway, wearing that little black pencil
skirt and the green blouse, black heels on her feet. My
favourite outfit. Her gaze was wary—clearly she still
remembered our argument from that morning.

Raising a hand, she pulled the hair tie from her ponytail, releasing her silky black hair down around her
shoulders.

My fingers itched to bury themselves in it, to take it
in my fist and pull her head back, kiss her throat, bite
her. Leave a mark on her smooth skin. I fucking *loved*

having my marks on her, showing the civilian world that she was taken, that she was mine.

But first things first.

I stopped pacing, thrust my hands in my pockets, curling my fingers around the ring box.

'Hey,' I said.

She sighed and came over to me, sliding her arms around my neck, rising up on her toes to kiss me. Christ, the way she did that, coming to me without hesitation... It gave me a thrill every time.

My heartbeat was revving like the engine on my bike by the time she pulled away, and when a crease settled between her black brows I knew she'd sensed my unsettled mood.

'What's up?' she asked softly. 'Is it about this morning?'

My mouth had gone dry and my pulse was out of control—which was insane. There was no reason to be such a pussy about this.

'There's something I need to say to you.' The words came out rougher than I wanted them to.

Cat blinked, then lowered her lashes—but not before I caught the spark of fear in her eyes.

'That sounds serious.' She took a step back and folded her arms.

Shit. She was doing what she always did when she was afraid. Retreating from me. Protecting herself. Which was *so* not happening.

I took my hands out of my pockets and pulled her back into my arms, keeping her little soft, warm body pressed to mine.

Her gaze widened. 'What's going on?'

Keeping one arm around her waist, I reached into

my pocket and grabbed the ring box, then held it out. 'This is for you.'

She glanced at the box, then back up at me, shock rippling over her features. 'Smoke, I—'

'Let me say something first. You told me this morning that you didn't want to think about getting a new place because this isn't supposed to be permanent.' I looked deep into those beautiful green eyes. 'Cat, this *is* permanent for me. When Justin finally gets what's coming to him, I'm not walking away from either you or Annie—get me? When I said I'd never leave you I meant it.'

She stared at me, not saying a word.

Not exactly the response I'd hoped for, but I made myself be patient. I'd had years to think about what I truly wanted from her, while all this—being with me— was still very new for her.

'We're not going back to the way it was before, kitten,' I went on, making sure she was absolutely clear on where I stood. 'Because I don't want to be your friend. I want to be more than that. I want to be your everything.'

Colour flooded her face, and I could feel her stiffen.

I didn't let her pull away, keeping my arm around her waist. 'Open the box.'

She hesitated, her reluctance obvious. I tried not to let it get to me. This would be a big step for her—especially given the shit she'd had to put up with in her last relationship. But I wasn't Justin and I'd told her that already. Surely she knew that?

She picked up the box from my palm and opened it. The ring I'd bought her gleamed on black velvet. It was silver; a delicate, stylised cat face, with pointed ears projecting out from the band and two genuine emeralds where the eyes should be. It had cost shitloads but I didn't care. She was worth every cent.

At least her reaction was what I wanted. Her mouth opened, and a surprised sound escaped from her. I could see that she didn't want to take the ring from its box and yet her hand reached for it anyway, as if she couldn't help herself.

I grabbed the ring before she could, though, because this was something I wanted to do. Gently I took her left hand and slid it onto her finger.

The fit was perfect, like I'd known it would be, and the emeralds glittered in the fading light coming through the windows.

'Smoke…'

Her voice was hoarse and she didn't look at me, her attention all on her hand.

'I don't understand. What does this mean?'

'What do you think?' I gripped her chin, turning her face towards mine. 'You're already my old lady, but the civilian world needs more than that. I want to make you and me legal. And I want to adopt Annie, be her dad for real.'

Emotions flickered across her face, too fast for me to read. But I got at least one loud and clear: *fear*.

She tried to pull away, but I wasn't having it. I'd told her she wasn't going to get any distance from me and I'd meant it.

'What are you afraid of?' I demanded, searching her expressive face. 'I thought you trusted me.'

Her hand pushed at me. 'Let me go.'

'No.' I gripped onto her jaw so she couldn't pull away, trying to ignore the hollow feeling in my gut. 'You've been happy being mine for the past two weeks—I know you have. So why is making this permanent a problem?'

'Smoke.' She pushed again.

I didn't move. 'You think I don't know you're scared? You think I can't see it in your eyes?'

Her hand pressed harder against my chest.

'You don't understand. Two weeks ago you were just my friend, and now suddenly you're putting a ring on my finger and telling me you want to make it legal. You're in my bed and in my life, and… Jesus, it's all happening so fast. *Too* fast. I can't…think.' Her eyes darkened. 'I need some time. I need some space, okay?'

A part of me understood that for her all this *was* fast. But that didn't stop the gut punch of disappointment.

I wanted to argue that over twenty years of friendship didn't make this 'fast', then crush her mouth beneath mine, take away her fear, give her pleasure instead. Make her see that all she needed was me.

Instead I let her go, taking a step back, giving her the space she wanted.

She sucked in a breath, straightening her back and lifting her chin. Then she slid the ring off her finger and put it back in the box, closing the lid and setting it on the coffee table.

The hollowness in my gut got wider, deeper. It felt like she'd reached inside my chest, put her fingers around my heart and squeezed it tight.

'You don't like it?' I couldn't keep the demand out of my voice, disappointment making it sound harsh.

Cat had folded her arms again, as if she was protecting herself against me, and her gaze was full of a hurt I didn't understand.

'I don't like it,' she said thickly. 'I *love* it. The ring

is beautiful and that's the problem. This is everything I ever wanted, and yes, that's…scary. Because I've wanted stuff before and it all went horribly wrong.'

The pressure around my heart eased. Okay, so she *did* want this after all. She wanted *me*.

'The past doesn't mean shit.' I tried to resist the urge to grab her again. 'And nothing's going to go wrong—not if I have anything to do with it.'

She glanced away, running a hand through her hair. 'You don't know that. Every single relationship I've ever had has gone bad. Every single one. And every time that happens, I lose.'

Her gaze came back to mine and this time she didn't hide her fear. It was there in her eyes.

'I'm tired of losing, Smoke. I'm tired of being left with nothing. My friendship with you is the only thing I have that hasn't gone wrong.'

I wanted to go to her and take her hand in mine, be the caring friend I used to be. But disappointment and frustration were eating away at me like battery acid. It felt like everything I'd always dreamed of was just within reach, and yet she kept pulling it away.

'I won't stop being your friend just because we're sleeping together.' I couldn't keep the harsh note out of my words. 'It won't change what we have now.'

She didn't look away this time. 'It's not change I'm scared of. I'm scared of getting in too deep. I need to have something left if this doesn't work out.'

'Why the fuck do you think this won't work out?'

My temper began to slip out of my grip, no matter how hard to I tried to keep hold of it, and frustration was gouging a ragged hole inside me.

'I've been your friend for over twenty goddamn

years, Cat, and I'm still your friend now. That's never
going to change. I don't know how many times I have to
say it. I don't know what else to give you. I don't know
what you want from me.'

Her mouth tightened, her green eyes dark. 'I don't
know either.'

I couldn't stand still any more—couldn't have this
distance between us. A distance that felt like it was getting wider with every passing second.

She put up her hand again as I moved but I ignored
it, grabbing her hips and pulling her hard against me,
pressing my rapidly hardening dick to the heat between
her thighs.

'So fucking think about it, then. What do you need?
Do you need to hear the *I love you* shit? Is that what
you want?'

A green flame leapt in her gaze and her temper answered mine. 'So *I love you* is shit? Is that what you're
saying?' She shoved at me. 'Fuck you.'

I knew I was making things worse, but I couldn't
seem to stop. All I could feel was that distance opening up and I didn't know how to close it.

'But is that what you *want*?'

I slid my hands over the curve of her butt, digging
my fingers into her softness through her skirt, flexing
my hips so my cock pressed harder against her groin.

'You want me to tell you I love you?'

Her mouth compressed, as if she didn't want to say it.
But I knew anyway. That was exactly what she wanted.

Love. What the fuck did it even mean? Not a goddamn thing. Love was a woman dying in a hospital bed
from the injuries her husband had given her. Love was

a backhand across the face and a cigarette ground out against bare skin. It was years of pain, years of abuse.

'Love *is* shit, Cat,' I went on roughly. 'And you of all people should know that. But this…?' I flexed my hips again, grinding against her, making her gasp. 'This is fucking *real*. This means something. Everything I give you, everything I do for you, means something. But, Christ, if you want the words so you can feel safe, I'll give them to you. And if you want to walk up the aisle in a fucking white dress, with bridesmaids and all that other crap, then you can. And if you want to stay in this shitty apartment then, sure, we'll stay in this shitty apartment. Anything and everything, kitten. Just say the word.'

The flush in her cheeks deepened, the flame in her eyes getting hotter. Her fingers had curled in the cotton of my T-shirt and the tension had gone from her muscles. She was moving with me now, her body softening against mine, because even if her mind was having problems accepting me that greedy pussy of hers had no such issues.

'What if I want to go back to being friends?' Her voice had got husky. 'What about that?'

'No.' I pulled her up on her toes, the length of my aching dick pushing against her clit, making her inhale sharply. 'No fucking way.'

Her gaze had gone even darker, the way it did when she wanted me badly.

'Then…you h-have to give me time.'

Jesus. Even when she was turned on and ready to fuck she wouldn't give one goddamn inch. I loved that about her, but it was driving me crazy right now. All I wanted was for her to say yes. To be mine, to choose me. Was that really too much to ask?

I knew how to convince her, though. Use our chemistry. Pull up her skirt and play with her pussy until she was sobbing and ready to give me anything I wanted. But I'd been hoping she'd say yes without that.

The battery-acid feeling was fire in my gut, with anger and disappointment and frustration all joining the party. Making me want to punch something. Or preferably fuck something.

Fine, if this was the way she wanted to play it, I'd play.

And I'd fucking win.

I was already hauling her skirt up, my hands sliding over the silky skin at the backs of her thighs, when my phone started buzzing in my back pocket. I knew the ringtone. It was Keep—which meant I couldn't ignore it.

Cursing, I let Cat go, but kept my gazed locked with hers as I dragged my phone out and answered it. I wanted her to know that this shit wasn't done—not by any stretch.

'What?'

I made no effort to be polite, because what was happening between me and Cat was important, and I'd already had one meeting with Keep today.

'I need you to come to the clubhouse for a chat,' Keep said shortly. 'Got a complaint from the cops about you.'

I scowled. That didn't make any sense. I stayed out of the cops' way and they stayed out of mine.

'What the fuck? I don't know what—'

'Just get here, Smoke,' Keep interrupted and disconnected the call.

Anger and thwarted lust simmered inside me. I could still feel Cat's heat against me, and the last thing I wanted to do was go back to the clubhouse and have a 'chat' with my president. But ignoring an order from Keep wasn't a good move, so I stuffed my phone back in my pocket.

'I got to go.'

Cat was already smoothing her skirt down, her hands shaking as she did so. It made a part of me savagely glad that even after two weeks of being in her bed I still had the power to affect her like that.

'Oh?' she said huskily. 'What's happening?'

'Club shit.'

I took a step towards her, hooked an arm around her neck and brought her in for a deep, hard kiss.

I lifted my head. 'This isn't over, kitten.'

Then I left.

CHAPTER SEVENTEEN

Cat

AFTER SMOKE HAD GONE, I sat down on the couch, my legs too shaky to hold me up. My heart rate was going through the roof and the heat of Smoke's hands lingered on my thighs. I could still feel the pressure of his cock against my throbbing clit and see the searing intensity in his dark eyes...

I took a breath, glancing at the little box on the table. The ring was perfect. Beautiful. I loved it. No one had ever got me anything so special and so completely *me* before. I wanted to put it on my finger and never take it off.

But I couldn't.

The past two weeks with Smoke had been amazing. He'd always been such a huge part of my life that I'd expected nothing to change. Yet somehow everything had changed.

He helped with Annie, talked with me, laughed with me, supported me the same as he always did.

But when night fell he didn't leave.

Instead he took me to bed. Made me scream into my pillow as he systematically explored and then destroyed every single one of my inhibitions—until there was no part of me that remained untouched by his mouth, his fingers, his cock. There was nothing I wouldn't let him do. He overloaded me with pleasure until I forgot why I'd ever been afraid in the first place.

Then there were those moments out of bed, when he'd put his hand on my back or thread his fingers through mine. When we'd be watching TV and his arm would come around me and I'd rest my head on his chest. Little touches, small reassurances.

I loved those. I hadn't realised how starved I'd been of them. Every time he touched me I wanted to arch into his hand and purr like the kitten he kept calling me.

Far from hurting our friendship, our physical relationship had only deepened it, made it richer. Made it into something really, really good.

And yet...

I stared at the ring box. I don't know why what he'd said, what he wanted from me, scared me so much. I should trust him, and I did, but the thought of putting on that ring made our relationship feel permanent in a way that wearing his property patch didn't.

Of course that was what he wanted, but the horror of my parents' relationship and then falling for Justin and having him hurt me so badly had hardened something inside me. I wanted to protect myself at all costs— protect my heart from the pain when everything went wrong, because it always did.

I wanted to protect myself from falling in love again, making myself vulnerable to someone who could hurt me. And Smoke *could* hurt me. He had the power to rip me apart without even lifting a finger, and that made him far more terrifying than Justin in every way.

Did I really want to give him that kind of power? Especially when he already had so much?

You're not exactly powerless yourself.

Well, that was true. I'd seen the disappointment in his eyes when I took the ring off and put it back in the box. He'd wanted me to say yes—that was obvious. And I couldn't deny that a part of me was perversely glad that somehow I'd managed to cause him pain, because I felt like he held my heart in the palm of his hand while he kept his own safely locked away.

'Love is shit, *Cat.*'

He would think that. Love for him meant everything bad, same as it did for me. But was he right? Were those words I wanted to hear make everything better? Would they make me feel safe? *I love you.* I didn't know. I *did* know that I didn't want him to say them to me just because it was what I wanted to hear. I wanted him to say them to me because that was what *he* felt.

Did he *actually* love me? Or was I simply a possession to him? Was I simply his property, like his bike or his cut? He did all these things for me—but was that because he'd do the same for anyone he considered his, or was it because of who I was to him?

How can it be you? You're not that special, remember?

The thought was hateful, so I pushed it away and got to my feet. I couldn't think about this right now—not when I had to go and collect Annie from the sitter.

I was in the hallway, ready to leave, when a knock came on the door.

Too busy thinking about Smoke, and what I was going to say to him when he came back, I didn't check the peephole, simply pulled the door open.

'Hi, Cat,' said Justin.

Everything inside me froze. My ex was standing there in his expensive suit, his slightly overlong brown hair expertly styled, looking handsome and success-ful, with his I'm-a-hell-of-a-nice-guy smile plastered on his face.

Taking advantage of my shock, he pushed his way inside, shutting the door firmly behind him. I took a couple of steps back before I could stop myself, my body instinctively remembering the shock and the pain of his blows and wanting to avoid them. Then I halted, furious with myself for backing away.

'What the hell are you doing here?' I tried to keep my voice steady. 'I didn't invite you in. Get the hell out!'

'Nope.' Justin shook his head, still smiling. 'I want to talk to you first.'

'Yeah, well, I don't want to talk to *you*. Get the fuck out of my apartment.'

He raised his hands in a calming gesture. 'Five min-utes, Cat. Give me five minutes.'

I didn't want to, but short of shoving him out through the door—and I didn't want to get that close to him—it didn't look like I was going to get much choice.

Folding my arms, I lifted my chin. 'Five. Then you're gone.'

He let out a breath, as if relieved, and ran a hand through his hair, that smarmy grin he thought was so charming curving his mouth.

'Okay, look… I've been thinking about Annie, and custody, and all that stuff. And how you're kind of trapped here in this…' He looked around, his lip curl-ing. 'Well, it's not exactly the best place for a kid, huh?

Anyway, I wondered if you'd consider maybe getting back together again.'

All the air in my lungs abruptly vanished, making it difficult to breathe.

'You're joking,' I managed. 'Please tell me you're joking.'

Justin's grin faded, a glint of heat entering his blue eyes. 'No. The truth is I miss you, Cat. And I want you back.'

He could *not* be serious. He couldn't.

'Are you insane?' I didn't bother to hide my shock. 'Why the hell would you think I'd *ever* want to come back to you? After what you did to me?'

His gaze flickered. 'I'm different now. I promise. And anyway it's better for Annie that we're a family. She needs a father.'

'She already has a father.'

The words came out before I could stop them. Because, of course, she did. She had Smoke. And he was a better father to her than Justin had ever been.

A mistake to say it out loud, though.

All the charm slid right off Justin's face like a switch had been thrown. The heat faded from his eyes, to be replaced by a hard, cold glitter. 'That biker asshole is *not* her father. *I* am. And if you care anything for her you'll know that her place and yours is with *me*.'

'Sure—with a man who can't control his own anger.' I didn't hold back the sarcasm. 'Who'd rather hit me than talk to me. Yeah, she'll be safer with you, all right.'

Justin's features rearranged themselves, the charm oozing back again. 'Oh, come on. You're really going to keep holding that against me? I loved you, Cat. I still do. Doesn't that count for anything?'

I stared at him—at Justin with his smarmy smile and his handsome face. Who'd told me he loved me countless times. And it hit me hard—like a brick to the side of the head—that, yes, he'd given me those words and I'd lapped them up, desperate for love and acceptance from someone.

But although the words had been what I wanted to hear, his actions had told a different story. When we were together he'd criticise me constantly, undermining me, making me feel that I wasn't good enough for him, that I had to work to be worthy of him.

He hit me.

He hurt me.

He made me feel small and weak.

But Smoke didn't do any of those things. No, he hadn't given me the words I'd been wanting to hear, but everything he did was for *me*. He built me up…made me feel beautiful. Made me feel strong. He was constantly pushing me, challenging me, making me step up because he knew I could take it. And he wanted the best for me. He wanted more for me.

Because he cared.

I could feel the truth of it sliding down inside me, imprinting itself into my blood, my bones. Into my soul.

He loved me. He might not have said it, but every day he showed me in the way he touched me, looked at me. In the way he cared for Annie. In every way there was.

And just like that my fear vanished.

I dropped my arms to my sides and took a few steps forward, getting right up in Justin's handsome, smarmy-ass face.

'No,' I said calmly. 'It counts for exactly zero. Because you don't love me, Justin. You never did. If you had, the last thing you would have done is treat me like shit, the way you did.'

He snorted, drawing himself up as if to emphasise his height, trying to make me feel small and weak.

'You're still pissed about a couple of slaps across the face? Come *on*. They didn't hurt that much.'

I don't know what came over me then—a tidal wave of rage, a firestorm burning away my fear and my vulnerability, burning away my weakness. I lifted my hand, drew it back and punched him in the face. *Hard.*

He reeled back in shock, blood pouring from his nose, and even though my knuckles were throbbing, it was the most satisfying sight in the entire world.

'What the fuck?' His hand went to his nose, his face going red.

'What are you getting so pissy about?' I asked. Rage was making me shake. 'It was just a little punch in the face. It didn't hurt that much.'

'You're fucking *crazy*!'

I took another step towards him, and it was even more satisfying to see him take a step back. 'You know the difference between you and Smoke, Justin? *Everything*. Every fucking thing. He's a better friend, a better lover, a better father. And he's sure as hell a better man than *you'll* ever be.'

Justin's face twisted and he reached out to grab me, yanking hard on my hair as he pulled me close. 'You crazy bitch. I'll teach you a fucking lesson about who's the better man.'

I wasn't afraid of him when his hands turned painful, ripping at my blouse, jerking up my skirt. Instead I was made of rage. I could feel it turning hot, burning bright, and I gathered myself, ready to explode.

Then suddenly Justin's hands were gone from me and the hallway was full of a harsher, deeper voice roaring, 'Touch her again and I'll fucking *kill* you!'

Smoke was there, and he'd grabbed the back of Justin's suit, hurling him into the wall so violently Justin bounced off it. Then Smoke closed in again, punching Justin in the face. Once. Twice. Justin fell to the floor, groaning, but Smoke hadn't finished. He kicked him in the ribs—a hard, driving blow. And again. And again.

My anger had begun to seep away, fear taking its place.

Smoke's face was a mask of rage and I knew without a doubt that if I didn't stop him he'd kill Justin—or put in him in the hospital at the very least.

I flung myself at Smoke's back, pulling on the leather of his cut. 'Stop it, Smoke! He's not worth the effort—he's not!'

But Smoke didn't listen. His boot was connecting with Justin's ribs again and again.

Trembling, I slid my arms around his lean, rock-hard body and laid my head against his back, letting him know that I was there.

'Stop,' I said hoarsely. 'Please, Smoke. *Stop.*'

I could feel the heave of his chest and the shake in his muscles, the intensity of his rage. It was like the rage that burned in me. But there were better ways of letting it out than battering a man to death.

Hell, I shouldn't have hit him myself—but then I owed him one.

I held on tight to Smoke and eventually he stopped, standing over Justin's groaning body, his breathing fast and harsh in the enclosed space of the hallway.

I thought that maybe it was too late, that we'd have

to call an ambulance, but eventually Justin moaned and rolled over, climbing slowly and painfully to his feet. His face was a mask of blood, his hand curled protectively over his ribs.

'You're fucking *dead*,' he said viciously to Smoke, his voice thick and mangled. 'No court in the state will give custody of Annie to her now. Especially not when I have you up on assault charges.'

He spat blood on the floor.

'Have fun in jail, *prick*.'

Then he turned and limped out through the door.

CHAPTER EIGHTEEN

Smoke

I WAS SO angry I couldn't see straight. People talk about a red rage and that was exactly what came down over my vision when I opened the front door to find fucking Justin tearing at Cat's clothing and pulling her hair.

There'd only been one other time I'd lost control of my temper so completely, and that was when I found Dad kicking Mom, over and over.

I'd shot him then, fucking up my life completely. Just like I'd fucked it up now.

I could feel the inescapable truth of it coiling and twisting inside me, and rage burned like rocket fuel in my bloodstream.

I should never have touched Justin, should never have punched him, but all I'd seen was his hands on my kitten, hurting her the way he always hurt her, and all I'd been able to think was that he had to pay.

She held me now, her arms around my waist, the warmth of her body against my spine, and that was what pushed back the red haze.

Too late, though. *Too fucking late.*

Justin had me now. He'd press charges, and since

Keep wouldn't want his good relationship with the cops put at risk I'd have to take some jail time. Especially since I'd disobeyed Keep's direct order and laid a hand on the police chief's son.

That would leave Cat and Annie unprotected, since there was nothing Keep could do legally to stop Justin from claiming Annie. Illegally he could, but I was betting he wouldn't want to deepen the shit with the cops that I'd already dumped him in.

Fuck.

I'd lost it for the club and I'd lost it for Cat, too.

I should have known that call from Keep was bullshit. As soon as I got back to the clubhouse he mentioned that the police chief had called through some complaint from a cop about me and he wanted me to explain. Easy enough. I hadn't even been in the city at the time, and Keep knew that because he was the one who sent me out of it in the first place. I realised in that moment that someone was screwing with me and it could only be one person. *Justin*. He'd made his father put through that call to get me away from Cat.

I'd headed straight back to her place immediately, riding like a fucking maniac, only to find that asshole with his hands all over what was mine. So I'd hit him and hit him, and now I was completely fucked.

And what made everything worse was that I knew there was only one way to fix this. Only one way to give Cat any chance at all of keeping Annie. Because she wasn't going to lose her—not because of me.

'Smoke?'

Cat's voice was soft, her fingers spreading out over my stomach, making my dick twitch.

'Are you okay?'

Jesus fucking Christ. I'd ruined her life and all she wanted to know was whether I was okay.

Abruptly I couldn't bear her touch—not when I knew what I had to do and how badly it would hurt her. So I pulled her arms from around me, making sure I was gentle and not the raging, violent animal I was inside, and stepped away.

'Smoke?'

I didn't want to look at her. All it would take for me to lose my nerve would be one glimpse of those big green eyes, so I kept my back to her and turned in the direction of the bedroom, moving towards it.

'Smoke.' She sounded sharper now. 'What's wrong?'

I stopped, but didn't turn. 'I screwed up.' My voice sounded like I'd just come back from a three-day drunken orgy. 'I screwed up totally. I'm sorry.'

'You mean the assault charges? You were protecting me. I'm a witness. I'll tell them that he was going to—'

'It doesn't matter what you say.'

I stared hard at the bedroom door, my knuckles throbbing from where I'd punched that cocksucker in the face.

'It doesn't matter what he did. No one's going to give you custody of Annie while you have a violent biker for a boyfriend.'

My chest hurt—a deep ache, like I'd been stabbed with a rusty knife.

'No.'

She said it like the word was all she needed to make it true and her hand was there again, settling between my shoulder blades, warm as the sun on a summer's day ride.

'We have the club. That's why I became your old lady to start with, right? They'll help us.'

'Yeah, I've fucked it up with the club, too.'

I could feel blood on my knuckles, could feel it drip down over my skin. A reminder of my past…of who I was. The ache in my chest deepened.

'Keep was real clear that I couldn't touch Justin because we had to stay sweet with the police. He won't be happy if that asshole presses charges and it makes it difficult for him.'

'But once you explain—'

'Explanations won't matter. All I can do is take responsibility for it and accept the consequences.'

Cat's hand was gone from my back and suddenly she was standing in front of me, her dark brows drawn down, her eyes full of worry. Then I noticed the tears in her blouse and the red marks on her skin from where that bastard had touched her. All the rage came flooding back.

'He hurt you.' My voice was guttural, making me sound like the fucking rabid animal I was.

'No, he didn't. I hurt *him*, in actual fact.'

'Your shirt…'

I reached out to touch the delicate material, fighting to keep myself together with the pressure of my fury crushing all the sense out of me. I wanted to put my hands on her, cover the marks Justin had left on her with my own. Reclaim her as mine as thoroughly and completely as possible.

Cat's attention dipped to my hand and she let out a soft breath. 'Oh. You're bleeding.' She reached for me.

No. Jesus. I couldn't have her touching me. Not now.

I lowered my hand and stepped back.

Her eyes widened. 'Smoke?'

It felt like that rusty knife was cutting a hole in my chest, peeling back my skin, pulling my ribs apart. I had to do this and do it fast.

'I can't stay.' Pain bled into my voice, no matter how hard I tried to stop it. 'I can't be with you any more. Not if you want to keep Annie.'

She blinked. 'What do you mean, you can't be with me any more?'

'I mean if the courts see you with me you're screwed. You're going to lose Annie. And the club won't save you—not now I've fucked with Justin. Keep needs his relationship with the cops and he won't want to put that at risk if Justin has me up on assault charges. I'll have to take the rap for it. I'll have to go down.'

'You mean jail? No, don't be stupid. You're not going anywhere—let alone to prison. There are plenty of other ways we can—'

'There are *no* other ways.' I cut her off harshly. 'You'll never get to keep Annie if I don't go.'

'But when you say you'll go, how long are you talking about? Just until this is over, right?'

That knife in my chest had turned into an animal, clawing at my guts, tearing me to shreds inside. I'd nearly killed a man in her hallway—would have killed him if she hadn't been there to stop me—and I was dripping blood all over her carpet.

Now she might lose her daughter because of me.

Now she might lose *everything* because of me.

She'd been right not to wear my ring. Right to take it off and put it back in that box. Right not to give me what I wanted. Right to be afraid.

I was dangerous. I hurt people. I killed people. And

one of these days, no matter how hard I'd try not to, I'd hurt her. Shit, I already had. I changed our friendship, forced her to be my old lady. She hadn't wanted any of that and yet I'd insisted.

What kind of man did that to a friend?

You know the answer to that, motherfucker.

'No, Cat.' I had make myself say the words. 'When I say I have to go, I mean I have to leave you. For good.'

She paled. 'What?'

'I can't be with you any more. It's better for you and it's better for Annie if I'm not in your lives. I'll take a jail term for the club if I have to, but I'm not having you or Annie connected to that. Not if it means you losing her.'

Her mouth had dropped open and she was staring at me like I'd turned into a stranger. 'You can't mean that.'

I held her gaze, letting her see the truth. 'I mean every fucking word.'

Green sparks of anger leapt in her eyes. 'No,' she repeated. 'You're not going to jail just because you were protecting me. And you're not leaving me. Just *no*.'

Of course she was being stubborn. Of course she was going to make this even harder than it was already.

'You didn't want this anyway, remember?' I couldn't help pointing that out. 'You wanted some time to think about it.'

Those green sparks leapt higher, her chin lifting in challenge. 'I know what I said. But what if I was wrong? What if I *do* want it after all?'

Oh, Jesus Christ. Please don't say she'd changed her mind. I couldn't deal with that—I just couldn't.

'Well, it's too late now,' I said harshly. 'This is the way it has to be.'

Not waiting for her to respond, I sidestepped her and headed into the bedroom.

I didn't want to have this discussion. Not with her standing there with that look in her eyes. Anger and, beneath it, pain. Not when everything I said would only make her angrier, cause her more hurt.

It was better I just go. Make the moment quick, like ripping off a Band-Aid.

In the bedroom I grabbed my duffel bag, then went to the dresser where Cat had cleared out a couple of drawers for me, taking out my clothes and stuffing them in the bag.

'You bastard.'

Cat's voice came from behind me, low and shaking.

'You don't get to do this. You don't get to change our friendship, make me want you, tell me you'll never leave me and then walk away.'

Each word hit like a bullet, opening up a thousand holes inside me, their edges jagged and ripped, my entire fucking soul pouring out through them like blood from a fatal wound.

'It's better this way.'

I kept my teeth clenched against the agony, balling up a T-shirt and shoving it into the bag.

'Better for who? For me and Annie? Or for you?'

The raw note in her voice hooked into the anger that was already boiling away inside me, making it sizzle like water on a hot exhaust pipe.

I turned around sharply.

She was behind me, her expression furious, her green eyes bright with hurt.

'You really want a man like me?' I demanded, unable to shut the fuck up. 'I'd have killed that fucker if you hadn't been here. I'd have beaten him to death for touching you.'

I took a step towards her, wanting to intimidate her so she'd back off.

'Is that the kind of man you want in your life? The kind of man you want around your daughter?'

Strangely, the look in her eyes softened, as if she could see something in me that I couldn't.

'This isn't about Annie and me, though, is it?'

I stiffened as she took a step forward, apparently not giving a shit that I was enraged and in pain and ready to smash something into oblivion.

She lifted a hand to touch my face. 'This is about you losing it with Justin. About your dad.'

Her gaze was sharp, opening me up, and I grabbed her wrist to stop her from touching me before I could think better of it.

'No.' I tried to ignore the warmth of her skin and the race of her pulse beneath my fingers. 'That shit's got nothing to do with this.'

I was lying, though, and we both knew it.

I'd killed my Dad and that ghost wouldn't *ever* fucking die.

Cat didn't move. 'You know what I thought back then, and that hasn't changed. You shot your dad because you were trying to protect your mom. And you beat the hell out of Justin because you were trying to protect me. You're a protector. *That's* the kind of man you are, Smoke. That's the kind of man you've always been. I thought you knew that.' She took another step closer. 'Being near Annie and me hasn't bothered you before. So what's changed? Is it Justin? Is it me?'

She was so close I could smell her familiar scent. It

was getting me hard. The tear in her blouse didn't help either, revealing the curves of her delicious tits.

Fuck, I wanted her so badly.

My grip tightened on her wrist and I felt her pulse begin to accelerate.

What had changed? *I* had. And she was the one who'd changed me. Being a friend was easy—there was a distance in that. But being more than a friend was different, and I hadn't realised 'til now what that meant.

Justin had not only shown me the truth of what I felt for her, he'd also shown me the truth of what I was inside. I was violent. Possessive. Territorial. I wanted to make Cat mine in every way, and the thought of her even touching another man filled me with murderous rage.

She didn't deserve that. Annie didn't deserve it either. Cat needed a man who wasn't controlling or jealous or demanding. And Annie needed a father figure who wouldn't lose his temper and beat to death some asshole simply for touching his woman.

'It doesn't matter what's changed.' I stared down into her beautiful eyes. 'Fact remains that me leaving is better for Annie, and that's who you should be thinking about right now.'

An intense expression flickered across her face. 'That's not true. You leaving is *not* better.'

She put her free hand on my chest, the warmth of her touch seeping through my T-shirt, making me *so* fucking aware of exactly how far away she was from me and how much I wanted to close that distance. Making the pain that was ripping me apart even worse.

'And what's good for us is you staying here. Because

you're good for *me*, and what's good for me is good for
Annie—can't you see that?'

I wanted to see it. I really did. But I couldn't. Not
when I'd never been good for anyone in my entire fucking life.

Unable to resist the urge to touch her, I let go her
wrist and took her face between my hands, cupping
her jaw. 'I've made my decision. I'm sorry, kitten. This
is how it is.'

Her mouth tightened, fury glowing in her eyes. 'No,'
she said. '*No.*'

And before I could avoid her she rose up onto her
toes and pressed her lips to mine. Kissing me.

I struggled not to respond. Every muscle in my body
was tight with the need to grab her, push her down on
the floor. Bury my aching cock in her tight little pussy,
make all the pain and the rage disappear.

But that would only make things worse.

And yet Cat was obviously hell-bent on making this
as hard for me as possible, because when I didn't respond
she pushed her tongue into my mouth, tasting me, kissing me as demandingly and as desperately as I'd ever
kissed her.

It was the hottest fucking thing I'd ever experienced.

She'd never been aggressive like this with me before,
never been this hungry. Like she was suffocating and
the only way to breathe was to put her mouth on mine.

My dick was like iron in my jeans, and I knew if I
didn't put a stop to this now I wouldn't be able to. And
then walking away from her would be next to impossible.

So I buried one hand in her hair and fisted it, trying to pull her head back. She resisted, making me

pull harder, which had to hurt her, yet she didn't make a sound when I finally managed to yank her away. Her eyes were huge and dark and full of rage, and I felt like my chest was made of nothing but broken glass.

'You can't leave,' she said furiously, before I could get in a word. 'I won't let you.'

Her hands reached down as she spoke, sliding over the front of my jeans, cupping my aching dick through the denim.

'I've changed my life for you and you don't get to walk away like that doesn't mean a goddamn thing.'

'Don't.'

I twisted her hair in my grip, some part of me wanting to hurt her for making this so difficult. For making this as painful as it was possible to get.

'Let me go, Cat. Just fucking let me go.'

Tears started in her eyes, but she ignored me, squeezing me instead.

And something in my head exploded.

I was angry, hard, and hurting like a bastard. Violence was humming in my blood. And she was so close, touching me, messing with my head, and all I could think about was showing her how wrong she was.

Showing her that it would be better for all of us if I wasn't in her life.

If she really wanted to know what kind of man I was, she was going to find out.

Right now.

CHAPTER NINETEEN

Cat

HIS HAND IN my hair hurt, but that was nothing compared to the pain in my heart.

I looked up into Smoke's beautiful face and saw my own agony reflected in his gaze along with the rage I'd seen as he'd launched himself at Justin.

That rage was mine, too, because I knew what had changed. Why he'd wanted this relationship to be permanent only to change his mind a couple of hours later.

Beating Justin up had brought back old memories. Memories of his father's death and his own role in that. And sure, that was hard. It wouldn't ever go away. But surely he knew what happened all those years ago didn't define him? That it didn't change my feelings about him?

He couldn't leave me. He couldn't alter our friendship forever, tell me I was his, promise me he'd always be there, only to walk away.

He couldn't make me fall in love with him, give me everything I'd ever wanted, only to take it all away.

I knew what he was going to do because I knew him. I could read it in those searing dark eyes as he bent me back over his arm, winding my hair around his wrist, making my scalp prickle with pain.

'You're going to try and distance me, aren't you?' The words were shaky and rough as he lifted his hand to the front of my blouse. 'You're going to try and show me exactly how bad you are for me. How much you could hurt me.'

He said nothing, his mouth closing on my throat, his teeth grazing my skin.

I trembled. Then trembled harder as he simply tore my blouse straight down the middle, the fabric sagging open.

'You're forgetting something,' I went on, my voice getting ragged as he nipped at my throat. 'I know you, Dane Kingsolver. I've known you since you were seven years old. And you've never once, not in twenty-odd years, ever been bad for me.'

Again he didn't reply, grabbing the delicate lace of my bra and jerking hard.

My bra ripped apart, and then his big, hot palm was cupping my bare breast, squeezing it, shaping it, his thumb flicking over my rapidly hardening nipple. I gasped, pleasure arrowing through me, getting sharper as he bit the side of my neck. Then he pinched my nipple—hard.

The pain made my eyes water, yet at the same sent a jolt of excitement right through me. A throb had started up between my thighs and when he pinched me again, twisting my nipple in his fingers, I felt that same jolt deep in my pussy, too.

He pulled my hair harder, arching my back and pressing my body to the furnace of his, lifting my breasts so he could bring his teeth there, too, licking the aching tips. I squirmed against him as his hot mouth closed around my nipple, sucking rhythmically, nipping at it, biting at it.

My breathing had become ragged and I was shaking, and then he yanked my skirt up, his fingers sliding into the lace of my panties, grabbing a handful of the material and tearing them away as easily as if they were tissue paper. Once they were gone his fingers pushed between my thighs, sliding over the bare, slick flesh of my pussy, massaging my clit roughly.

Pleasure cut me like a knife.

'Smoke… Oh, God…' My voice was as ripped and torn as my clothes.

His scorching dark gaze was on mine as he slid one finger into me, keeping his thumb pressed hard to my clit, staring at me as another finger joined the first, pushing deep. Then he separated both fingers, stretching me, making me groan and tremble and burn. Crushing me with pleasure.

I knew what he was doing. He hadn't wanted me to fight him so he'd taken control, the way he always did. But I couldn't let him do that—not today. He was trying to leave me and I'd be damned if I let him go. I couldn't stop him physically—not when he was so much stronger than me—but, as I'd learned over the past couple of weeks, I wasn't exactly powerless.

I knew what his weakness was.

Me.

I looked up into his face as his fingers worked in a short, hard rhythm that made my hips lift and jerk, building the pleasure relentlessly.

He wasn't untouched by what he was doing. I could see the black flame in his eyes, the darkness burning, searing. The lines of his face were taut and hungry, something like a snarl twisting his beautiful mouth.

I stared into that heated darkness, let myself melt into him.

Maybe he knew what I was trying to do, because he pulled his fingers from my body and brought them to my mouth, shoving them between my lips, a feral look on his face.

'Lick them,' he ordered. 'Taste how wet you get for a fucking killer.'

I obeyed, keeping my gaze on his as I licked his fingers, tasting my own musk and the saltiness of his skin. Tasting *us*. Together.

There was strength in resistance, but sometimes true power lay in surrender.

'I love you,' I whispered, falling into his midnight eyes. 'I love you so much.'

Anguish flooded his face and suddenly I wasn't bent over his arm any more but turned to face the wall, shoved up against it, his hot, hard body coming up behind me, pinning me there. I turned my face to one side, the texture of the wallpaper pressing into my cheek and against the stiff points of my nipples, making my breathing wild and my heartbeat stampede in my head.

He put his arm against the back of my neck, keeping me jammed to the wall. His short, ragged breath was in my ear.

'Those words mean nothing.'

There was a whole world of pain in his voice.

'Don't ever fucking say them.'

'But they mean something to me,' I gasped out. 'I don't want you to leave. I love you and I—'

His palm covered my mouth, stopping me from finishing.

I didn't struggle. I let him keep his hand there. Because not being able to say the words didn't change the intense rush of feeling in my heart.

But I shuddered as I felt him nudge my feet apart, knowing what was coming next. Wanting it. Craving it more than my next breath.

I heard his zipper being pulled down and then his lean, powerful body covered mine, worn denim and warm cotton against my bare back, his free hand reaching around to spread me open, the long, hard length of his cock pushing inside me.

We hadn't bothered with condoms since I'd gone on the pill, and I shivered at the feel of his hot skin against my slick flesh, at the exquisite stretch and burn as he slid deeper, filling me. Impaling me.

I whimpered against his palm, the pleasure of him inside me making me arch against him, wanting more, wanting him deeper still.

'Fuck… *Cat*…' His whisper was desperate, and I felt him turn his face into my neck, the hand over my mouth sliding down to grip my throat in a possessive hold.

His free hand reached for the back of my knee, lifting my leg up, spreading me wider for him. Then he pressed his palm to the wall with my knee hooked over his wrist, opening me up, his cock pushing so deep I shook.

He began to fuck me hard, each thrust powerful, crushing me between the wallpapered surface at my front and the furnace heat of his body at my back.

I should have tried to protect my cheek from the rough scrape of the wallpaper. But I didn't. I simply relaxed against him and let him do what he wanted, gave myself to the grip of his hand on my throat and the feel of his cock slamming in and out. His breath was hot against the back of my neck as he slid the hand on the wall up, lifting my leg higher, spreading me even wider. Then he adjusted his stance, thrusting up hard enough to lift me onto my toes, tilting my hips and making my back bow, penetrating me even deeper.

A choked sound escaped me as his rhythm picked up speed. The hand on my throat tightened, making me short of breath and light-headed.

But I wasn't afraid. I would never be afraid of him.

'There's nothing you can do to push me away,' I whispered. 'There's nothing you can do that I won't want. There's no part of me that isn't yours. And even if you leave me I'll still be here for you. I'll always be here for you.'

'Don't say that.'

The raw anguish in his voice made my heart clench tight.

'Don't say that. *Please.*'

He thrust harder, faster, moving the hand around my throat down between my legs, his wicked fingers finding my clit, stroking me firmly, making the words mixed up in my head and my thighs shake. Making me pant like a dog as the orgasm rushed towards me and then crashed over my head, screaming Smoke's name as I came.

His thrusts became wild, and then he slammed into me one last time, his teeth sinking into my shoulder as he came, too, the raw sound he made loud in my ear.

I was too dazed to move for long moments after that, content to stand there with the heat of his rock-hard body at my back and the warmth of his breath against my nape.

But then I remembered what he'd been going to do and I squirmed, making him drop the hand with my leg hooked over it so I could stand. I turned, pushing at him because he was leaning heavily against me, wanting to see his face. Wanting to kiss him. Wanting to hold on to him before he tried to leave again.

His dark eyes met mine and for one long, aching second I thought I'd won. Then he looked away and I knew I hadn't won after all. I'd lost.

Despair opened up inside me and I reached for him. But he'd already pushed himself away, stumbling back as he adjusted his clothing. His face was a mask, unyielding as stone.

But I wasn't stone. I was nothing but exposed nerve endings.

'Don't go.'

I couldn't hide my desperation. If I'd had the strength, I would have tried to grab hold of him, but the wall was the only thing holding me up.

'I'm sorry,' he said emotionlessly, turning away and reaching for his bag.

'You said you'd never leave me.' The pain was sharp in my voice, but I didn't care. 'You said you'd always be there for me.'

'Yeah.'

He headed towards the door and didn't stop.

'I lied.'

Then he was gone.

CHAPTER TWENTY

Smoke

I RODE BACK to the clubhouse on autopilot, parking my bike and ignoring whatever the prospect at the door said to me as I strode inside.

I was vaguely surprised that I wasn't trailing blood everywhere, because it sure felt like I was bleeding to death. Like my heart had been ripped from my chest and all that was left was a bloody hole.

My head was full of Cat, full of the wet grip of her pussy around my cock, the soft give of her body as I shoved her against the wall. Full of the rapid beat of her pulse as I put my hand on her throat.

Full of her voice telling me she loved me. That she'd never leave me.

I'd been shot once or twice before, and that was nothing compared to the agony I was feeling now. Walking out through that door had been like ripping myself in two.

But what else could I do?

She hadn't listened to me—hadn't done anything but relax into me as I'd torn her clothing and nearly choked her. As I fucked her hard and deep against the wall. I wanted her angry, wanted her fighting me, but she wasn't and didn't.

She just…gave me everything.

And you flung it back in her face.

Ignoring the sound of my stupid damn conscience, I headed straight for Keep's office for the third time that day. Brothers nodded to me, saying, 'hey', but I ignored them, too. I didn't have the time or the patience for meaningless fucking chitchat.

'Jesus Christ,' Keep said as I entered the office without knocking, coming to stand in front of his desk. 'What the fuck is it *this* time?'

I put my hands in my pockets and came straight out with it. 'I beat up Justin Grant. Smashed his pussy-ass face in. So now he's going to press charges. I just want you to know that I'll take full responsibility and that—'

'Shut the fuck up,' Keep snapped, glaring at me. 'Again. From the top.'

I gritted my teeth, violence simmering inside me, itching to get out.

'That bullshit call from the chief? It originated from Justin. He wanted me out of the house, so he could get to Cat. That's what I found when I got back home. Him with his hands all over her.' My rage boiled over. 'So I taught him a fucking lesson about not touching what's mine.'

Keep sat slowly back in his chair, his gaze sharp. 'You couldn't have kept better control of yourself?'

My jaw ached, every muscle in my body tight. 'Funnily enough, when he was tearing her clothes and hurting her, controlling myself wasn't uppermost in my fucking mind.'

Keep said nothing, continuing to stare at me.

'Like I said,' I went on, since it didn't look like he was going to break the silence, 'the asshole's going to press charges and he'll sure as hell make sure Cat won't get custody of Annie. So I'm here to tell you she's not my old lady any more and to that I'll plead guilty. I'll do the time.'

Keep scowled. 'What do you mean she's not your old lady any more?'

'I can't stay with her. Being with me is only going to hurt her.'

There was a dull throbbing in my chest—a low-level pain that wasn't ever going to go away.

'I only made her mine because I wanted the club to protect her anyway.'

Keep snorted. 'What a fucking load of bullshit. You made her your old lady because you're in love with her—everyone knows that.'

That word. Christ, why did everyone keep saying that word?

'It's not like that. It was fake. It was supposed to protect her and—'

'Yeah, and that's bullshit, too. You've been in love with that girl for as long as I've known you, and that's a fuck of a long time. And she loves you, too. Jesus, the way she looked at you at the party that night, it was written all over her face.'

I said nothing, every part of me tense with denial.

My uncle shook his head slowly. 'You fucking idiot. Why did you leave her? And don't give me that shit about protecting her.'

'I had to.' I could feel a muscle jumping in the side of my jaw. 'I nearly beat to death the father of her child. What kind of role model does that make me for Annie? Fuck's sake, Keep. Cat already ditched one violent asshole—she doesn't need another.'

Again, Keep stayed silent. Then, after a while, he said, 'You're a lot of things, Smoke. But I didn't think being a little bitch was one of them.'

My hands clenched into fists in the pockets of jeans, rage surging through me. 'Sorry, Keep, but you say that again and, president or not, I'll smash your god-damn face in.'

The bastard just laughed.

'Oh, come on. Admit it. You're not leaving Cat to protect her. You're leaving her to protect your own worthless hide.'

The ground felt suddenly uneven under my feet, my gut lurching.

It's true. You know it's true.

No, it couldn't be. I wasn't that much of a fucking coward, was I?

Keep cocked his head. 'What are you so afraid of? What do you think she's going to do? Leave you? She's been your friend for years. She knows all your skeletons and yet she's still here.'

'How can I be with her?'

I hadn't meant to say it, but it came out all the same, raw as a gunshot wound.

'I killed your fucking brother and I nearly killed Grant. I'm no good, Keep. You know it. I know it. Cat needs to know it, too.'

'And you're full of it. David earned his death and I don't blame you for it—you know that. All I know about Cat is that you've been a good friend to her for over twenty years. You love her, and you love her kid, too, and I know you'd die to protect the both of them. What more needs to be said?'

He paused.

'Whether she wants to be with you or not is her decision, and if she wants you—well, shit… Who are you to tell her she's wrong? And don't give me that crap about not loving her. Giving her up is killing you. I can see it in your face.'

My jaw ached—everything fucking ached.

'I don't deserve her.' My voice didn't even sound like mine. 'She's…everything I'm not.'

Keep sat forward and leaned his elbows on his desk. 'Of course you don't deserve her. That's why you're gonna spend every goddamn minute of your life making sure you do.'

I stared at him. My uncle, my president. The man who'd been more of a father to me than my own dad ever had been.

'It's not just Cat.' The words were as rusty as old nails. 'I screwed up with the club, too.'

Keep's blue eyes were very direct. 'What the fuck kind of club do you think I run? Think I'd let a piece of shit like Justin Grant take a good brother down?' One corner of his mouth tilted up. 'I've got your back, Smoke. You should know that.'

The raw, aching wound in my chest throbbed. 'What I did is going to make—'

'Leave me to deal with the club. You go deal with your woman. And for fuck's sake do it quickly—because I can only imagine what your drama's doing to her right now.'

I couldn't move—just stood there frozen.

Of *course* the club had my back, and so did Keep. How had I forgotten that?

Like you forgot Cat had your back, too. She always did.

A hot, painful feeling shifted inside me. Shame. Remorse. For the way I'd walked out on her. For forgetting everything she'd done for me. For forgetting twenty-three fucking years of friendship.

Twenty-three fucking years of love.

Keep was right. I *did* love her. I loved her with everything in me. And I'd been as big a pussy as Justin to leave her the way I did. Because I was scared of how much I wanted her. Of how much she meant to me. Horribly afraid I wasn't worthy of her and never would be.

Except there was no reason for me to be such a goddamn coward. Cat had never rejected me—not once. Not even in the terrible aftermath of Dad's death. Every single time she'd been there for me when I needed her. Without judgement. Without criticism.

She loved me.

'Even if you leave me, I'll still be here for you. I'll always be here for you...'

Her voice echoed in my head and the pain was more than I could bear.

'Thanks, Keep,' I said hoarsely. 'I got to go.'

Keep sighed. 'About fucking time.'

CHAPTER TWENTY-ONE

Cat

I PICKED ANNIE up from the sitter and brought her home, gave her dinner and a bath, tucked her into bed, trying to act like nothing was wrong. Like I didn't have an empty hole in the centre of my chest where Smoke had ripped out my heart and flung it onto the floor, grinding it into nothing under his heel.

I didn't know how I was going to manage without him in my life. He'd been my friend for so long that I couldn't imagine him not being there. And the past couple of weeks, when he'd been more than just a friend... God, thinking about *them* only made the loss more painful.

I loved him, but for some reason that wasn't enough, and now he'd gone.

Once again I'd lost everything.

It hurt so much.

I knew eventually I'd pull myself up and start again, like I always did. Find my feet and get my life back together again. Figure out what I was going to do about Justin—all that shit. But right now it felt like it was all too much.

Right now all I wanted to do was cry.

I sat on the couch with a pillow in the time-honoured fashion, curling around my pain. And then I saw the ring box sitting on the coffee table, and that sank the knife even deeper into what remained of my heart.

It was all I had left of him, that ring. He'd taken everything else.

I reached for the box, opened it and looked down at the little cat face with its glowing green eyes. It was perfect. *So* perfect.

A tear slid down my nose, splashing on top of the silver band, making the eyes sparkle.

Had my taking it off pushed him over the edge? Was that why he'd walked away? Perhaps if I'd left it on, everything would have been different and I wouldn't be sitting here, sobbing on my couch with my heart in pieces.

The sound of the front door's handle turning came suddenly from out in the hallway and my whole body went cold. No one but me had a key, and unless Justin had somehow managed to—

The living room door slammed open, bouncing on its hinges. Smoke stood in the doorway.

And I found there must be something left of my heart after all, because it was racing and throbbing and hurting. And my body wasn't cold any more, but burning hot.

Smoke's dark gaze found mine, and the look on his face was searing in its intensity.

I opened my mouth to say something, though I had no idea what.

I never got the chance. Because Smoke strode over to where I sat and before I even understood what he intended to do he swept me up into his arms, and his mouth was coming down on mine.

It was a hungry, desperate, demanding kiss. It was hot and it was raw, and when I tried to pull away, he gripped me hard, holding me still. Kissing me and kissing me and kissing me, as if he was afraid to stop.

All I could do was let him devour me, with my hands pinned to the hard wall of his chest, feeling the frantic beating of his heart against my palms matching my own.

It felt like forever before he finally lifted his head, staring down at me with those familiar dark eyes. Full of heat. Full of desire.

'I was such a fucking coward, Cat,' he said hoarsely. 'I should never have walked out on you. I'm sorry. I'm sorry for hurting you. I'm sorry for not listening to you. I'm sorry for turning my back on you.'

He lifted his hands, cupping my face, his thumbs stroking lightly along the side of my jaw, making me shiver. Making me tremble.

'But most of all I'm sorry for being such a little bitch and not telling you how I feel.'

I couldn't speak. My throat was too tight—every part of my body was too tight. I didn't want to move in case this was a dream and he'd vanish, leaving me being held by nothing but empty air.

'I thought I was protecting you,' he went on, his voice dark and ragged. 'But I wasn't, kitten. The only person I was protecting was myself. Keep put me straight about a few things and that was one of them.'

'Why?' I finally managed to ask shakily. 'What did you need to protect yourself from?'

'What do you think?'

He looked down at me as if I was the only thing worth looking at in the entire universe.

'I was protecting myself from *you*.'

I stared at him in shock. 'Me?'

'There's no one on this entire planet who has more power to hurt me than you do. You could fucking destroy me with a snap of your fingers.'

His thumbs moved over my skin, a gentle back-and-forth movement, raising goosebumps everywhere.

'I've loved you for so long. So fucking long. And then Justin made me lose it, and… Well, I guess I was looking for an excuse to run the hell away. I'm not worthy of you, kitten. You're the most perfect woman I've ever met and I'm just a violent biker with a temper and a really shitty past.'

I swallowed, trying to get past the lump in my throat. 'So why did you come back?'

'Because you were always there for me. Because you never let me down. You had my back, Cat. You always had my back. And I thought that if you'd stuck around for twenty-three years, it must be because I wasn't such a lost cause after all.'

That beautiful mouth turned up into one of his rare, heart-stopping smiles.

'Plus, Keep said he was going to kick my ass if I didn't come straight back here and make it right with you.'

I took a shaking breath. 'Wait… You said you love me.'

'I did. I do. And no, before you say it, it's not because you want to hear the words. It's because that's what I feel every time I look at you.' His smile deepened. 'Turns out love *does* mean something after all.'

It was only then that I had the courage to lift my hands from his chest and touch his face, run my fingers over the rough stubble along his jaw, check that he was real and this wasn't a dream.

'You know you don't have to deserve me, don't you? You only need to keep doing what you've always been doing. Being my friend.'

Something in his eyes flared hot. 'Oh, kitten. I'm sorry, but I don't want to be your friend any more.'

'Then don't be,' I murmured and slid my arms around his neck. 'Be my husband instead.'

Much, much later, as we lay naked on the floor of the living room together, our skin streaked with sweat and our bodies sated, Smoke opened the ring box and took out the ring. Then he held my hand in his and looked into my eyes.

When he slipped the ring onto my finger, he didn't ask me to marry him. Instead, he asked, 'Will you love me, Cat?'

I didn't need to answer. He knew what I was going to say. But I answered him all the same.

'Always, Dane. With all my heart.'

EPILOGUE

Smoke

I DON'T KNOW how Keep did it in the end, but he got Justin to drop the charges. The prick also dropped his custody suit, leaving me free to adopt Annie. Which I did the first moment I could.

It turned out Cat *did* want to walk up the aisle in a white dress—*and* with a goddamn bridesmaid. I could hardly refuse, especially since I'd promised her she could. We even had a flower girl—a job Annie took very seriously.

I'm not a big fan of weddings, but I have to say that mine was the best ever. I even got a bit fucking misty when Cat came down the aisle towards me in her wedding dress, her big green eyes staring at me from behind her veil.

So damn beautiful.

She made my heart ache.

She taught me that *love* isn't just a meaningless word. That it's deeper and richer and more powerful than I ever imagined.

She was my friend, my lover, and now she was my wife I didn't think life could have got any more perfect.

But it did.

It sure as hell did.

* * * * *

LET'S TALK
Romance

For exclusive extracts, competitions
and special offers, find us online:

f facebook.com/millsandboon

🄾 @millsandboonuk

🐦 @millsandboon

Or get in touch on 0844 844 1351*

For all the latest titles coming soon, visit
millsandboon.co.uk/nextmonth